LEGENDS OF COLORED TRESSES

BY: IVAN CERDA

Legends of Colored Tresses

Print ISBN: 979-8-89786-008-1

eBook ISBN: 979-8-89786-009-8

CONTENTS

PREFACE:

History, as it has been taught, is accurate. Well, at least date-wise. (Depending on perspective and involvement, the details will vary.) One small detail ignored or not mentioned is the hair color of the historical protagonists or antagonists. We, as a society, assume hair color. The reality is that hair color as we know it didn't begin to evolve until the mid-sixteenth century in Japan and the late eighteenth century in England. These tales tell the story of the origins of hair color. Each color expresses characteristics of its originator, which marks a legacy for those honored with having the same.

Humanity had the same hair color, white. This is not to say that those with white hair are any less important or don't possess any worthy characteristics. We must understand that no matter the hair color, we all return to the beginning: white hair. But will we have white hair as an honor (a sign of wisdom and grace) or as a curse (a sign of complacency and mediocrity)? These tales share stories of the lives of the originators of hair color.

It is important to note that boys and girls with the same hair color as any of these characters share the same traits. Some may have more, and some may have less, but the spirit and heart of each main character may be shared by many.

DISCLAIMER:

These stories are based on a period and culture with a more beautiful, powerful, and fantastic history than described herein. The inspiration for these tales does not impose ideology or represent these communities in any way. It feebly depicts the respective regions only to enhance and shape the storyline. Please read history's deep and powerful stories for more accurate details on the Vikings, the Irish, the Englishmen, the Samurai, the Shoguns, the Japanese, and the Mexica.

DEDICATION

Thank you, friends, and especially family, who have always supported me in everything I wanted to accomplish. Dad, Mom, Vero, Vanessa, and Val, I greatly appreciate and love you.

To the dreamers and imagination wranglers: go for it! You never know what you are capable of accomplishing.

TALE I
EMBER RED: KEERA

In the verdant embrace of Ireland's rolling hills was a modest wooden home, sheltering a father, a mother, and their daughter Keera, aged seven. A lush patch of land overtook the front of the house that bloomed with vegetables and flowers, while behind it, a creek cascaded from distant lands towards a tranquil lake. As the morning sun painted the world in golden hues, the clouds above danced, mirroring the swaying grass caressed by the gentle breeze.

"Bang!" The sound came from the front door, which opened and slammed shut. Keera ran out of the house. Through the garden, she darted, her fingertips brushing the leaves of many plants. Skipping to the backyard, her bare feet relished the cool grass as she twirled joyfully.

Her white, shoulder-length hair pirouetted across her face and rosy cheeks. After a whirlwind of circles, she leaped onto a tree stump, arms raised, before landing back on the earth. Brimming with wonder and curiosity, her emerald eyes scanned the landscape, eager for the day's unfolding adventures.

Meanwhile, within the cozy confines of the home, Keera's parents, Felíc and Ava, sat at the kitchen table. The home felt warm, not just from the sunlight that beamed through the windows, but because this house exudes comfort, love, and family. Felíc's coffee cup shifted between his hands, mirroring the thoughts that swirled within his mind. Ava leaned forward, grasping Felíc's wrist gently, drawing his attention. Their gaze met. Though sharing Keera's emerald eyes, their hues were clouded with worry, a heaviness dimming their once-bright spirits.

"He will be back again snarling for payment of the land," Felíc said, "He came by twice last month."

The "he" Felíc referred to was a deviant, pompous landowner: Cormac.

His height didn't match his ego, and his face resembled something you would never want to see again. He was a wealthy man who owned much of the land along the creek and even some around the lake; he continually lorded it over people. His dealings with young families seeking a home were shrouded in deceit, promising far more than his terms delivered.

"We shall weather this storm as best we can. Expecting miracles from nothing is beyond reason," she reassured. Despite a bountiful harvest, prosperity remained elusive without a market to trade. Their table became a council chamber, echoing with plans and worries as they pondered the looming shadow of the debt collector.

Sitting at the table, their words began to form a plan. The more they spoke, the more the plan eased their worries and calmed their thoughts. Finally feeling some relief, rapping on the door made them jump. They stared at each other briefly, and then Ava stood to answer the door. She slowly opened the door with a trembling hand. There stood an unwelcome visitor. Cormac stood at their threshold, an embodiment of entitlement sprung to life.

Skipping pleasantries, Cormac began his hubris speech. "I just came to tell you...", At this point, Felíc came to the door, and Cormac continued, "Oh, there you are. I just came to tell you I will be back this evening expecting my payment in full. If not, you will need to find a new home. Thank you, have a good day". With a smirk, he departed, leaving behind an air of hopelessness.

Felíc put his arm around Ava, a shield against the harsh reality. She turned and nuzzled into his neck and began to cry. He reassured her and told her, "We will be ok." Keera, a silent witness to her parents' plight, approached cautiously, her innocent inquiry instantly changing the mood. With a heavy heart, Ava masked her distress with a facade of normalcy, protecting her child from the storm brewing around their sanctuary.

"Are you ok, Momma?" she asked.

Ava wiped her face on Felíc's shirt and responded, "Yes, honey. Momma and Daddy were telling each other how much we love one another and wondered where you were because it was time for breakfast."

Felíc frolicked around, feigning a chase to ensnare Keera and whisk her indoors. Keera, enchanted by his antics, found herself paralyzed by laughter, unable to resist. With gentle strength, Felíc scooped her up and carried her inside. The day seemed to Keera like any other day, and that is how Felíc and Ava wanted it to be. A child should never be bogged down with the troubles of adults. As hard as it is for parents, together, they can overcome many things because, as aides, they have their children's smiles to help them along.

The morning went by faster than usual. Felíc headed to the market to sell vegetables and herbs from the front yard garden. Though his produce was coveted, many of his regular patrons faced financial constraints due to political instability in town and across Ireland.

Other farmers, masons, and tradesmen felt the weight of the crumbling economy.

After only making a few sales close to the end of the workday, Felíc went home knowing his earnings and the money they saved would not be enough to appease Cormac. He pulled his wagon, still bearing some produce. Each heavy step pronounced the gravity of his worries, yet his resolve remained unshakeable. With sweat glistening on his brow, he trudged homeward, the wagon a mute testament to his toil. He walked up a hill, down a path, over the creek bridge, through a small hazel grove, along the creek, and over another hill to a field with a clear view of his home.

There, he began to smell Ava's Irish stew filling the evening sky like a perfume that instantly took him to a memory, a feeling. Like a key unlocking a door, the

scent unlocked a flood of warmth, trans-
forming his demeanor as he hastened
toward the beacon: home.

By the time he arrived home, the golden
sun had descended, painting the sky in
hues of orange and pink, a tapestry of
serenity. It was the most picturesque
scene—house, family, food, yard, creek,
and sky. Problems and difficult situa-
tions had no room here, and the fact that
Cormac's face hadn't scared the beauty
away calmed Felíc and Ava even more.
Laughter danced amidst the aroma,
mingling with the fading light as stars
emerged in the sky above.

With empty bowls and hearts full of
memories, Ava took off her Celtic Knot
Braided ring and led Keera to the far end
of the house for a bath. Ava smiled as
she watched Keera play in the tub. Felíc
took his boots off, untied the neck lining
of his léine, and sat at the end of the bed.
Hearing Keera and Ava laugh and play
enveloped him in comfort, bringing a
smile to his face.

Now cleaned and dried, Keera was taken

to the front room to allow Felíc to bathe. Ava took Keera to her bed, brushed her hair, and listened to her as she told her stories about the kids in her classroom. Ava, with exaggerated interest, interjected and asked questions. After discussing the latest classroom news, Ava kissed her forehead and said, "Sleep well and dream deep." Keera snuggled under the blanket and fell asleep.

Ava walked to the bedroom where Felíc was already out of the bath and in the room. He dried his hair by running his hand back and forth on his head. They looked at each other, took a deep breath, gave each other an encouraging smile, and then got ready for bed. They didn't want to speak or say a word. They didn't want to welcome thoughts that would steal their sleep. Instead, they both kept the sound of Keera's voice in their minds: the voice that calmed and en-couraged good thoughts.

The night was calm. The gentle breeze through the windows barely drowned out the babbling creek in the backyard. Then the faint sound of trot, trot, trot slowly slithered closer and closer. Trot, trot, trot. Louder and prouder, it sounded almost like a drum foretelling the approach of something ominous and vile. Trot, trot, trot. Even the breeze wanted to make itself scarce. Trot, trot, trot. On his beastly horse, there, by the gate at the end of the garden, rode Cormac. It was not that the horse was evil; instead, it was such a majestic horse, but its rider just defiled any lordly appearance.

"Felíc!", he shouted. "Wake up, Felíc; I'm here for what is mine." Instantly, Felíc sat up, grabbed his léine, put it on, and then walked to the door where his boots and brat waited for his use every morning. He walked out the front door.

"There you are. Must you keep me waiting?" Cormac snarled. "I want my money at this moment, or, like I said earlier, you will need to find a new house."

Ava walked out the front door and stood next to Felíc. Her left shoulder was behind his right. She grabbed his hand and, with the other, his shoulder. "I was able to go to the market and make more money. It's not the full amount, but I have some," Felíc answered in a restrained voice. It was a plea.

"I thought you might say that. Both of you come here. I want to see your faces better", said Cormac in an oily voice with a vicious smile. The couple approached.

Cormac pulled the reins, and the horse turned on the spot. Without explanation, a burst of orange and yellow flame appeared in Cormac's hand, and then it was thrown over Ava's and Felíc's heads toward the house. The tail of the fire looked like a speeding horse's tail headed toward evil deeds. CRASH! The vial of incineration shattered into pieces, and the wooden house was ablaze almost immediately.

Ava screamed and began to cry bitterly. Her knees weakened, and she fell. Ava's hands clasped on her lap, and tears poured out, making her face reflect the flames. Felíc turned and looked at Cormac, who sat haughtily on his horse. He ran toward him, "Why would you do this, you bastard?" demanded Felíc. Cormac pulled out his short sword and pointed it at Felíc. He immediately stopped approaching Cormac and said with a breaking voice, "My daughter is in there!" Cormac's face blanched a sickly white, if you could believe a paler color could exist, one almost matching his few strands of hair.

The roaring fire began to subside as thuds and crashes stifled what was left of the flames. Rubble, ash, and embers were all that remained. Felíc walked to Ava, who was still crying. He knelt beside her, hugged her, and tried to console her. Cormac regained his composure by shaking his head to start the blood flow again and return to his usual slimy persona. Cormac turned his horse to trot away when suddenly a tiny voice said, "Momma, what happened?"

Keera walked out of the horrific inferno's aftermath without a single burn on her body. But the most remarkable thing was that her hair still seemed on fire, glowing ember red. Fear came over Cormac as he watched the child with this glowing hair. He hit his horse with the side of his blade and galloped away.

Ava and Felíc, in shock, stayed where they were. Keera walked toward them. "Are you okay, Momma?" Keera asked.

Both Felíc and Ava touched Keera's hair and pulled her in for a much-needed hug filled with relief, awe, and a strange new sense of adventure.

In moments, the neighbors on either side of their now-destroyed house came running toward them to see if they were okay. As if rehearsed or seeming as if they had hit an invisible barrier, they stopped when they noticed Keera's hair. After shaking his head to clear his mind from surprise, Cillian, one of the neighbors, cried out, "Is everyone ok?"

"Yes, we're ok," replied Felíc.

Without asking or getting directions, the neighbors helped salvage and clear out the house. After about an hour, hugs and handshakes were exchanged. Cillian, along with his wife and two sons,

Deaglán and his wife, daughter, and son, promised to return in the morning to help them rebuild the house with what they had available. The story of what happened was asked to be repeated as they couldn't understand how it was possible, but the proof stood in plain sight. Cillian and Deaglán helped Felíc clear some debris to make a temporary room for the family to sleep. The flames affected Keera's room the least, so they decided to all sleep on Keera's bed.

The following day, still bewildered, neighbors came and helped Ava and Felíc as they stared and marveled at Keera's hair. It was never discussed, but it seemed agreed upon not to talk about the previous night's events to anyone else.

Felíc and Ava noticed something good had already come from this new marvel; Cormac wasn't seen or heard from that next day or for the next few weeks. Once in a while, he would slither out of his hole, but he never returned to the house by the creek. Ava and Felíc were genuinely grateful as they weren't pestered and hounded for payment. The red hair from nefarious deeds was now considered a good luck charm. This breath of fresh air cleared Ava's and Felic's thoughts while grounding them to face a new challenge the next day. Keera was going back to school.

Ava bathed Keera and tucked her in for the night after a day of repairing and rebuilding. She walked to the dining table and sat in front of Felic, who was once again deep in thought, his eyes darkened. "Should she go to school?" he asked.

"Of course she should; there's nothing wrong with her," responded Ava.

"The kids are going to stare, point, and laugh. The teacher might even send her back home", continued Felíc, ignoring Ava's comment. "Maybe if she wears a hat, or you can tie a handkerchief around her head," Felíc muttered as he looked up at Ava, who smiled at him. "Don't worry about her; she isn't worried. She said she couldn't wait to show her friends that she has 'fire in my hair'", said Ava with a smile and a face that was peaceful, calm, and assured. "You're right," he replied, "If she were able to get through this weekend, she could do anything." With those words, his thoughts eased, so they headed to bed. They knew they were going to have a good night's rest because now, there was nothing that could disturb their sleep.

The next morning was like any other school day for Keera. She got ready for school and ate breakfast. She acted as if she didn't know she had red hair, or it didn't make a difference that she did. Keera walked hand-in-hand with her mom to school. Her hair moved in the breeze, careless and free. The closer they came to the school, the more nervous Ava became. Ava decided to take the patch headdress from her pocket to hide Keera's hair as best she could. Ava pulled Keera back toward her and turned her around. The patch headdress did a very good job at covering Keera's hair. Once it was on, Ava took a deep breath and grabbed Keera's hand again.

They walked for another couple of minutes, and their journey's end came into view.

They stood outside the old wooden schoolhouse. Keera walked toward the schoolhouse door but was pulled back by her mom's hand, which still held her tightly. Keera looked back and smiled, "See you later, momma." Ava smiled back and slowly released Keera's hand. The confidence that Keera demonstrated eased Ava's worries a bit, well, as much as possible, because parents will always worry about their children.

Keera, not even considering her hair, walked into the classroom and took her seat. Her friends approached her and started conversations about what they did during the weekend and how they wished it were the weekend again. Amidst the talking and kids running around the class, Keera removed her headdress. All conversations stopped. The kids who ran around quickly got to their seats because they thought the teacher had entered the room. Looking toward the door and seeing no one, they looked around and saw the cause of the call for silence. Keera's face showed the same surprise as everyone else's. Neither understanding why the other reacted the way they had.

"It's good to see that the weekend did not erase the rules about how children should act in a classroom," said Mrs. Walsh. She continued, "Let's begin today by going over the..." Her voice trailed off as she noticed Keera's hair and her eyes repeatedly blinked to make sure her eyes didn't deceive her. Making light of the situation and seeing all the children still gawking at Keera, she struck the desk with her pile of papers, making the kids jump in their seats and face forward. Taking this as a sign of a return to normalcy, Mrs. Walsh started the day's lesson.

Throughout the day, the only two voices heard in the classroom were Mrs. Walsh's and Keera's. The children still couldn't decide how to process the red in the room, contrary to Keera's unchanged disposition. Lunchtime seemed like a midday show. The kids ate their food while staring at Keera, almost expecting something to happen. Her friend sitting next to her finally got the courage to speak after Keera looked over and smiled,

"Your hair is red".

"Yup," Keera responded matter-of-factly.

"How?" asked a boy across the table.

"I don't know; I woke up and heard my mom and dad crying outside. I saw fire all around me, but it wasn't hot. I got out of bed and walked outside to Momma and Papa. They grabbed my hair, then hugged me, and that's it", Keera responded. Eyes widened and mouths agape, the kids began to talk and ask more questions. By the end of lunch, things returned to a pre-hair day at school.

Mrs. Walsh wouldn't admit it, but she preferred the quiet class from the morning instead of what was happening now: the playing around, the infamous "Why"

question. This made her day go by
slower, but for the kids, the school day
was over before they knew it. They all
ran outside and made their way to their
houses. Keera walked outside and met
her mom, who waited for her on the dirt
path. Ava noticed that Keera's hair was
dancing freely in the afternoon breeze.
Trying to hide her worry, Ava asked,
"How was school?" With a smile still on
her face, Keera responded, "It was fun.
I think I have more friends now". On
the way home, Ava began to think about
Keera's hair. Why am I more worried
about this than she is? Do I dislike the
hair? Am I the type of person I am trying
to protect Keera from? These thoughts
ran through Ava's mind as Keera weaved
on and off the path through the grassy
field. They continued this way until they
reached the creek bridge. Then they
went through a small grouping of trees,
along the river, and over one last hill.

The sun in the sky, blazing down, made
it clear why the color of the grass was
fading and why Felíc worked hard on the
garden to keep it watered and tended.
His white hair in the sun, a beacon to

Keera, beckoned for a sneak scare. Stopping in her tracks, Keera's mind began to figure out the best approach. Through her focused eyes, you could almost see the wheels turning. Attack planned, she crouched and took sporadic skips and steps, catching her balance after some daring leaps. Closer and closer, she approached her target. Felíc, deep in concentration on whether he should water twice a day now and add more to the garden on the side of the house, didn't even notice the clumsy approach of his daughter. Of course, to Keera, it was pure stealth and skill. Felíc looked over his shoulder, and his eyes caught a glimpse of a dancing flame in the grass. Smiling, he pretended he hadn't seen anything and returned to work. Twigs and drying grass crunched underneath Keera's shoes. Her steps quickened, and struggling to hold back her giggles, Keera walked up behind her dad and, through a big smile, shouted, "I gotcha!" Felíc laughed and hugged Keera. Ava joined in, and then they walked into the house.

School seemed normal and more manageable for the remainder of the year. The kids made Keera the class leader, whether they knew it or not. The girls tried their best to be beside her, talking to her the most. The boys encouraged each other to talk to her. Mrs. Walsh gleamed when her classroom gathered with the other students and teachers, as she knew she had the poster child, the anomaly.

Math and reading were usually the focus of their daily studies, but during this school day, history was introduced. The story of Ireland is one of continual battles. Keera listened intently as Mrs. Walsh divulged the struggle and outcome of the Sack of Drogheda. Anger welled up in Keera's eyes, and her hair seemed to glow bright red. "This won't happen again?" asked Keera. "We can hope that it won't, but if lessons weren't learned, then something like this could repeat itself," answered Mrs. Walsh in a voice that reassured but also warned. Keera's heart beat steadily, wondering what it would look like to be in a place to make decisions that could shape a town, city, or even a nation. After all, a person either aided or deterred everything that happened in a region or country. Keera imagined herself as one of those persons: a vanguard, a pioneer, a leader.

Though they made other students' eyes roll, history lessons became Keera's favorite subject. Keera kept Mrs. Walsh on her toes, asking question after question and making suggestion after suggestion. "Do you think they meant for things to get that bad? Maybe they did it on purpose to have the people need them to help," Keera said as Mrs. Walsh explained King Henry VIII's self-declaration as King of Ireland.

"Am I Catholic?" asked Keera.

"Being Catholic isn't like being from somewhere, like calling yourself Celtic. It is what you believe," Mrs. Walsh said.

That evening, the questions continued at home. Felíc and Ava felt they were talking to a grown-up, not their soon-to-be eight-year-old daughter. "Yes, we are Catholic because we believe in God and the authority of the priesthood," answered Felíc to Keera's question.

"So, our garden isn't ours?" she asked.

Felíc and Ava stared at each other and gave a slight smile. "Yes, the garden we have is ours and the land around the house too," Felíc answered, still with a smile on his face, for he knew that Cormac wouldn't lay claim to the land again after he almost burned their daughter alive.

The older Keera became, the fewer but more complex the questions became. Nine, ten, then eleven: "Does a foreign monarchy benefit Ireland?"

Twelve, thirteen, then fourteen: "Why end feudalism if the societal classes we have known seem to mimic that failed idea of social structure?"

Fifteen, then sixteen: "Why can't I continue to study and learn? My beliefs shouldn't be a way to measure what they think I should know. It would benefit them to educate everyone who wants to be educated so better-equipped people contribute to building a better society instead of creating a society that depends solely on the decisions of others."

The church, the nobles, and just about everyone in town began to know the name Keera. It was, for the most part, associated with disrupting the peace (their peace) and undermining the rules and norms of society (their made-up, self-serving order). Keera's hair symbolized passion and courage to her and those who agreed with her point of view on change. In contrast to those who pursed their lips when they saw her, the hair was a banner of insubordination, disorder, and disrespect. The town's leaders did not know how she always knew when and where the council meetings were held. The term "fiery redhead" was coined in those meetings because not only was her hair a stark contrast to her white-haired contemporaries, but her speech and intellect seemed to lash out at the old-fashioned ideas of the supposed enlightened.

"How is it that a mere seventeen-year-old, and a woman at that, feels

she has the right to come to our meetings to lecture us about our experience
with juvenile idealism?" confronted one
of the members of the leading counsel.

"You are right to question my authority,
as I have not been allowed to study as
the rest of you have. Without permis-
sion but with pure passion and hunger
for knowledge, I sought wisdom, for she
calls out in the streets. I heard her call
and joined the desperation to satiate
the ever-seeking thoughts of curiosity
and progress. I stand here now. Yes,
I am young, but I have learned to the
capacity, not of someone in my ranks
but of an outranking intellectual. You
should be proud of this, for one of your
own can stand their ground and defend
themselves and their fellow townspeople's interests. When I speak, much to
the surprise of all listening, I do not do
so lightly, nor do I intend to belittle your
intelligence or downplay your experience. What I desire to present is a new
way of thinking and challenging the
process, not for the mere task of caus-
ing an uproar, but for the simple fact of
presenting other possibilities," answered

Keera in a voice steady and empowered by confidence. Her words ended the meeting.

The men seated at the table looked at each other and nodded as they began to leave the room. Keera stood there without words as, one by one, the men walked out. Keera did not know what to do. She took a deep breath and decided to leave the room as well. A gentle hand grabbed her arm. Keera looked back and saw a skinny man with thinning white hair about the same height as her. The man smiled and said to her, "That's true Irish blood in your veins." Keera smiled as tears filled her eyes because she now knew that her words had been heard and maybe, just maybe, she would be taken seriously in her passions and fight for knowledge.

Keera didn't let a moment go by without a question being asked or her opinions being made known. Such as the fire that consumed her house those years ago, she, too, wanted to consume everything she could. Not that she sought recognition or to be an inspiration, but she was still. Boys and girls her age began to follow Keera's example, and soon, the town and surrounding areas became the country's epicenter of politics, music, art, and ethics. And it all started with Keera as the spark.

TALE 2
NIGHT GLOW: ASTA

The cold air became still, and snow, though early compared to other years, began to fall on the ground around Asta. She sat by the shore, waiting to see the lights reflected off the shields of the Valkyrie as they ushered the fallen into Valhalla (to us, it's known as the aurora borealis: Northern Lights). Asta, a sixteen-year-old Viking Princess, always ensured she was ready to witness the lights. Her white hair, in a loose side braid, lay over a thick grey fur coat. Around her neck, a silver chain held her family crest: a round silver medallion with a raven diving straight down through the air. She grasped her silver chain in one hand. It seemed like she was reciting a prayer, or perhaps she thought the medallion was the way to open the skies to reveal the lights.

The night grew colder. She pulled her knees up to her chest and wrapped her coat around them as she leaned on a rock. Slowly, she dozed off, and in between the tiny slits of closed eyelids, she saw a glimmer. You know that space between awake and asleep, where you can still hear and see things from the world around you, but you aren't sure if it is a part of the natural world or the dream world, so you don't know how to react? This was the space where Asta found herself. If it was a dream, she wanted to go deeper into it to explore the lights, but if it was in the real world, she wanted to wake up and appreciate what was happening.

Asta's next heartbeat jolted her out of her slumber to tell her the wait was over. Now startled awake, Asta looked at the water and saw waves of beautiful green, blue, and purple sparkles. The glorious lights began their routine dance across the sky. They seemed so free, yet beautiful and stunning. It looked like the lights did what they wanted, moving as they wished. Asta's eyes moved quickly, scanning the water to avoid missing one color or movement. Then, in sync, the lights began to fade along with Asta. Her eyes became heavier with every blink. Soon, the lights were no more, and Asta fell asleep again. In her dream, she imagined that she was the light. Moving freely as they did, she would see new things in her journey across the sky: different people, lands, sights, sounds, smells, and tastes of an unknown world.

Asta enjoyed her dream. Then, from behind Asta, someone walked toward her. Step by step, the sound of snow being crushed underfoot became louder. A gentle hand touched Asta's shoulder; then it began to rub her head softly.

It was Astrid, Asta's mother. "Come to bed, darlin'. It's late, and it is getting cold out. A new day will start soon enough, and your father should be back early in the morning". Asta began to squirm and slowly wiggled to convince herself to get up. Asta got up and walked to her bed after a couple more insistent rubs and a bit of a harder pat from her mom. Pushing open the curtain of her room in the longhouse, Asta took off her boots, shed her coat, and slipped under a pile of wool and fur blankets. She quickly, once again, entered her world of adventurous travels.

The following day, Asta awoke from a deep, dream-filled sleep to men yelling and responding to orders, wooden ships creaking, and families walking toward the approaching voyagers. She knew the sound well; many a time, this sound caused joy in her as it marked the return of her father, Balder, and now her brother Bjartr, who made his first voyage. Quickly, she got up from her fur-laden cot, jumped into her boots, splashed her face with water, and ran out to where the boats would dock. As she approached the docks, she noticed everyone, including her mom, was already out, waiting. Walking onto the pier, Asta stood next to her mom. The great Viking ships at the end of their journey, the sails lowered, and the boats were tied to the dock. Down came a ladder, and with it came the brave men who had explored and conquered new territories. One by one, they come down. The last four to leave were Ulf, the second in command, with his son Kåre, who, like Bjartr, had just realized his first journey.

Kåre was a very handsome man with a strong face. His arms and chest were muscular, but his long, skinny legs seemed forgotten and left in their childhood state. He stood taller than his father, but his appearance was not nearly as demanding as his father's. Finally, the leading magnate disembarked, followed by his son. If you haven't guessed, these are Asta's father and brother. Both these men seemed regal. Though they could be seen as unkept and unruly, their persona and air were respectable. Unlike Bjartr's body, Balder's was thick and almost indestructible. His hair was weathered by age and the elements, tied up in a tight knot. This juxtaposed to Bjartr's, which blew freely in the breeze.

Each party was welcomed by their family with hugs, kisses, and a few arm punches from siblings. Slowly, each family returned to their longhouse. The only people left on the pier were Ulf with his wife and son, and Balder with his family. Balder began boasting about how great Bjartr and Kåre did on their first seafarer's journey as they shared stories and banter. "Any woman would be lucky to have either of these two as their husband," he added as he looked at Asta. She and Kåre blushed as Astrid said, "I think they both agree." All but the blushers laughed. Asta walked toward the shore off the pier to ease the awkward moment. Everyone else followed suit, off the dock to the village's center and into their houses.

Once inside, Astrid told the servants, "Make sure the food is done soon. Once Balder is done with his bath, he will want to eat a good, hot meal". With all that action in the kitchen, it didn't take long for Asta to walk outside to escape the bustling house. It seemed all the young daughters of the voyagers had the same idea. The communal fire pit was the meeting place to escape the hectic kitchens. It was also a place and time to wait out bathing voyagers. As they sat around the fire pit, glistening eyes, smiling faces, and perked ears marked the time. Everyone knew what this meant. It was time for one of Asta's stories:

stories of voyages, shipwrecks, encounters with other creatures, and exploring new lands. Of course, the tales she told the young girls were all make-believe because women were not allowed to sail with the men.

Nonetheless, the girls would envision the fantastical adventures depicted by Asta's imaginary tales. They, too, thought of a time when they could walk on an island and meet dwarves or sail up the coast and see the elves on the northern shores of the enchanted forest. All the girls huddled together around the unlit fire pit. Their mouths went from gaping to smiling, and they were surprised all in one story.

The story was interrupted by the mothers' calls, who said the food was ready. They all stood up and returned to their houses except Asta, who lingered a while longer. Unsure if she was beginning to believe her own stories or the fact that she thought it possible to have her own adventures, she whispered to herself, "Soon." She lifted her head and looked at the boats in the distance being rocked by the waves. She smiled, got up, and headed to her house.

Her father and brother were already eating when she walked in, so she sat at the table, and her mother soon joined them. The servants brought over their plates. In a nice big bowl was a hot vegetable soup, the last of the harvest safely in houses as winter was already at hand, along with fresh fish, freshly baked rye bread, and a large helping of buttermilk or ale. "Not as spectacular as my son, but that Kåre boy turned out to be a good Viking, wouldn't you agree, Asta?" Asta just looked up with a spoonful of soup still in her mouth.

"Yes," added Astrid, "and a very handsome man indeed; I could imagine the likes of the children he can produce."

Balder twisted his face to this as he didn't want to think about his daughter in that light. "You will be seventeen soon, and it will be time to settle down in your longhouse with a worthy Viking." Balder took a big gulp of his ale and continued, "Not just you but also

you, son." Bjartr looked at his dad arro-
gantly, "I already have someone in mind,
and I am sure her family will not protest.
It's an old jarl's youngest daughter, and
not to mention the best looking". Balder
nodded in approval. His head turned
again toward Asta, who was still trying
to avoid eye contact by sipping her soup
way more than necessary. Astrid cleared
her throat not to speak but to demand a
response from Asta. Bjartr leaned forward, putting his elbows on the table
and his hands clasped over his mouth to
cover his sneering smile, if possible.

Asta swallowed her nonexistent soup,
took a deep breath, and responded,
"Yes, you're right. Kåre will make a great
husband and father. We will just wait for
him to ask for my hand". She said this
because she knew Kåre to be yellow-bel-
lied when talking to girls. "It's settled,"
Balder said as he lifted one hand and
closed it quickly like he had caught
something or made a great deal. Astrid
reached to grab Balder's other hand on
the table, and they both smiled.

Asta's face showed a bit of confusion

and worry. "Kåre spoke to me last night before we all went to bed. He asked if I would approve of his and your union," said Balder, still smiling as he continued. "He wanted the wedding to be next year after we return from our voyage before winter begins. He and his father have already planned where to build the house, and they want to start as soon as possible".

Balder continued to speak, but the words in Asta's ears seemed warped, drowned out by her thoughts. I knew I had to get married, but so soon? I haven't even been outside of this village. I haven't sailed anywhere. And if I get married, I'll never be able to do anything else but... "Did you hear your dad, Asta?" Asta returned to her senses by shaking her head to shake out the thoughts that distracted her. "Uh-huh."

The next couple of months were a complete blur. Every day, there was a visit from either of Kåre's parents. Kåre would come by, but only to discuss house plans and finalize the layout with Asta. Ulf made it very clear he wanted the ideas and plans finalized by Up-Helly-Aa, so, at the first signs of spring, construction could begin. Besides the continual planning, winter seemed uneventful, so Kåre and Asta would make excuses to leave their houses and meet up anywhere to talk and distract themselves from the demanding decisions of their future married life. This everyday escape made it easy for them to talk to each other. The once-shy boy began showing interest in and liking for Asta. And Asta, always interested in Kåre, welcomed the blossoming young man. Usual talks were filled with personal jokes and flirtatious looks. They were becoming friends, partners.

Once, right before the Up-Helly-Aa celebration, Asta and Kåre stood next to the ship that would be burned. Asta asked, "Do you like sailing and coming back and sailing and then doing it repeatedly?" Kåre took a deep breath and answered, "I think I'm supposed to like it, and I do, but I don't know how long I can do it. Even though I have only been away once, it feels like I could do more if I could sail somewhere and stay there for a while, not just sack and loot and come back home."

"If you could do anything, what would you do?" asked Asta. Kåre smiled and responded, "I would still sail but sail south, dock wherever, and begin a life there. Explore the land, work the land, and build a house. And, if I wanted to sail again, I would just come visit family here and then head back to my land, my work, my life."

Asta smiled from ear to ear at this answer, and Kåre joined her. They felt something inside them, like an invisible rope that tied and joined their hearts. Kåre's pinky moved slightly to touch the back of Asta's hand. They stared at each other and somehow knew their life together would be adventurous. After being lost in the moment, which seemed like a long time, they stood up and went to the line of torches around the ship, where people began gathering for the ceremonial burning.

The following day seemed to bring warmer weather, which made Ulf a bit more annoying because he wanted Asta and Kåre to frame out the boundaries of their house to ensure the door was facing in the correct direction. Taking this as a chance to spend more time together, Asta and Kåre grabbed two large sticks and went to the plot of land already chosen for their house. Kåre held the stick and propped it up like a walking stick. He placed one hand on his hip, stood with his chest out and head slightly facing up, "What say you? What shall we call our land?"

"Frihet!" exclaimed Asta as she grabbed her stick with both hands and propped it up before her. "Ai, good choice. Now, where will the eyes of this land face?" retorted Kåre. Asta turned on the spot, pulled the stick from behind her, over her head, and pointed toward the bay, "In this direction." "Another good choice," Kåre responded with a smile.

With their house planned out, they drew lines in the snow. Walls, doors, windows, rooms, and a fence. They had their house before them etched out like a life-sized blueprint. They stood beside each other with their sticks. They marveled at their home. A nervous jolt pierced them in their stomachs as they realized this would be their home, together, in one place for as long as they lived. The lines in the snow weren't just containing the house; boundaries seemed to encompass their lives. They chose to escape reality and walked to Asta's home for an early lunch. The crunching snow underneath their feet seemed to be the only conversation. Not even the much-desired clear sky and sunshine could break the ice that held their thoughts captive on their forever home and stay.

After seeing them walk into the house, Astrid urged them to sit at the dining table to eat soup to warm them up. Both were still numb from the realization of life, so they sat and began to slurp their soup. Noticing something was wrong, Astrid brought some bread in a woven basket, sat at the table, and asked, "Are you guys happy with how your house will look?" Both smiled and nodded yes. "OK," Astrid continued apprehensively. "It's almost a year away from the wedding. Any more thoughts on that?"

Kåre looked at Asta for some relief from the inquisition. Asta responded, "No, nothing new. I think we will talk about it more in a couple of months. I think Ulf will have us busy supervising the long-house construction."

The words she spoke seemed to fall out of her mouth. The thought of "forever" still circled in her head like a vulture getting the scent of a carcass. Were her dreams the carcass and the house their coffin? Astrid stared at Asta because a few seconds passed without a word from her, but her mouth was open and ready to speak. "Well, I'll just wait to hear those details later." Astrid patted Kåre on the wrist, stood up, and entered the kitchen.

Were they thinking the same thing? The looks on their faces made it seem as if they were dazed, confused, unsure, or reluctant. They both knew that probably talking about it wouldn't be the best. So, after eating their lunch in silence, Kåre stood up, walked to Asta, kissed her on the head, and walked out of the house. No words were necessary to know they were both trying to make sense of the word "forever".

The endless vastness of the word snuffed the life out of any childish idea of marriage. Marriage seemed as alluring as death. Why would someone want to marry anyone if it meant being trapped in something you've been trying to imagine a way out of your entire life? The hot soup did not affect Asta. Not knowing how to deal with the thoughts and emotions, Asta dragged herself to her room and threw herself onto the cot. Maybe if I sleep a bit, it will be ok. After tossing and turning for most of it, an hour later, Asta got up, walked through the dining room toward the door, ignored her dad and brother at the table, and walked outside.

The cool breeze that started biting the skin a little didn't faze Asta. Her mind was overrun with emotions, conflicting emotions. The only logical thing left to do was cry. Cry because of what, for what? Now, she was confused about that as well. Without noticing, she was at the bay's shore. The water lapped closer to

her feet. Opposing. Conflicting. Wanting. Denying. Staying. Leaving. Loving.
Settling. Things seemed more manageable when there was just one, at least a
bit easier. Was life now a steady yes, in
one direction without looking around,
like a puff of smoke, in and out? Was
life now just joy felt when a decision
was made, and nothing was left for the
journey? Is this independence? Is this
marriage? Is this life?

The water now splashed against Asta's feet. The burst of cold froze her
thoughts. As soon as the thoughts
froze, she felt comforted and secure.
She looked down at her hand; Kåre was
holding it. They looked at each other,
smiled slightly, took a deep breath, and
stared into the horizon. Oblivious to
everything else, they stood there hand in
hand.

Time came and went. The snow melted,
the grass thickened, and the house was
built. Once again, Asta and Kåre were
hand in hand at the shores, this time for
a farewell. It was time for Kåre to make
his second trip and for Asta to prepare

to be a wife. This farewell felt heavy, weighted with everything at stake and weighted by what was to come. Sails filled with a strong breeze, the ships glided away until they had their fill of adventure and plunder.

Spring blossomed into summer. Summer burned into autumn. Autumn fell slowly. Asta made many walks to and around her house. Sometimes alone, but more often than not, with a company of girls helping to elaborate the stories of Asta the Adventurous. Welcoming the distraction, Asta encouraged their imagination and introduced them to her new land: Frihet. Moments like these hurt and soothed Asta's heart. The taste in Asta's mouth was bittersweet as the skies turned grey and the grass withered. Winter was blowing in. Days became shorter, and nights were longer. The Valkyrie prepared their welcoming parade.

This night was cold, but no snow fell. The voyagers liked to make it home before the snow began to fall. So, in this pointless cold, Asta sat down again to see if the Valkyrie would visit her. Waiting, she began to think of what was to come. Her new life was to start with Kåre, but would it promise many adventures? She did love Kåre, and they seemed to get along just fine, but she couldn't deny the emptiness that came over her when she thought of them being together in that house.

Would this be my life, she thought, spending most of the year just waiting for him to come home from being in far-off lands, discovering new things? Just waiting to have children, raise them, and then wait for them to get married. This "waiting," even just in thought, tired her. So she snuggled up to the rock, pulled her coat around her, and before she fell asleep, a smile came on her face, erasing all other thoughts, and she whispered, "Soon." Whether she said it longingly or spoke out of hope is unknown, but "soon" approached.

She closed her eyes and slept. The village seemed to have joined her in slumber, as a stillness was all around. It was like the stillness lulled everyone to sleep.

It was as if Skadi was rocking them to sleep by singing a wordless lullaby. As Asta slept, the most remarkable thing happened. This is unknown to all except for us, as I will tell you about the events that followed, for it was too magical not to tell. The auroras began their ever-increasing dance across the sky as she leaned on the rock. Strand by strand, color by color, they moved and waved over the tranquil but oblivious village. Much like a choreographed dance, the dancers, though beautiful and free, remain within the confines of the choreography; the lights usually did the same, but this time, they moved a little closer, and they seemed to even dance on Asta's head.

Every ribbon of green, blue, and purple was like a brush stroke of pure color on her head, almost golden, like the color of the light's source. Movement by movement, Asta's hair became increasingly golden, beautiful, and radiant. When the dance was finalized and the lights began to dim, remnant glimmers of light seemed to be on her hair. Slowly, they faded to reveal sunlit hair.

She slept there all night. She didn't feel the cold, nor did she get cold. Besides sharing their freedom and beauty, the lights warmed her throughout the night. But, much like last time, the following day heralded commotion. The creaking of the boats, the jostle of the people walking to the pier, and laughter and conversation did not stir Asta. It wasn't until Balder asked for her that everyone began to look around; no one more hastily than Kåre, as they were to be wed in two weeks.

After a few moments of searching, a young girl shouted, "Over here!" Though only two words, they were filled with such definitions: joy, confusion, wonder, and awe, to name a few. When her family and soon-to-be family arrived, the entire village surrounded her. People began to whisper:

"What's wrong with her?"

 "Do you think she looked at the lights directly?"

"I think it's beautiful."

"It's an omen, I tell you!"

Balder and Astrid knelt on either side of her, and Astrid began to call her by name as she rubbed her shoulder and face. She was nervous at first because she did not understand the meaning of what she saw. Slowly, Asta's eyes opened, and her expression was as con-fused as the onlookers. She sat up, and a few people stepped back.

"Are you ok?" asked Astrid.

"Yes, I just think I fell asleep outside; that's a first," Asta giggled.

Her parents helped her up, and more people took a step back. "What's going on? Is Bjartr ok?" Asta asked hastily. "I'm okay," answered Bjartr in a tone that asked, "But are you okay?" Astrid reached out and slowly grabbed a ten-dril of Asta's hair. It felt warm, and this sensation made Astrid's hand quickly re-tract like she had received a slight shock.

"Does it hurt?" she asked.

Asta, settled in confusion, and after a few blinks to ensure she was awake, responded, "Does what hurt?" Kåre walked up to her with eyes that looked upon Asta, not with fear or confusion but with affection, awe, and love more than before, if this was possible. He grabbed her hand, and with the other hand, he touched her hair. He felt the warmth of it but didn't let go. He felt warmth rush through his body, and his heart beat slower but stronger. Asta looked at her hair in Kåre's hand and saw what caused everyone's stares. Asta was lost in Kåre's eyes, not caring about it, which said I am with you and will go with you wherever you go; you are mine, and I am yours.

With tears welling in her eyes, Asta pulled Kåre in for a deep hug. Some people gasped, still unsure what to make of the situation. Young girls giggled and fought the urge to clap and cheer. After this sweet embrace, Asta stood beside Kåre, firmly holding his hand.

"I want to move the ceremony and have it in two days. I want to marry Kåre. At the first sign of spring, I want to sail with him to the south to make our own life and have our adventures." Her words made the girls smile, and their eyes filled with wonder. It was as if they saw the dancing lights right in front of them, moving and glowing brighter and brighter. Balder was about to speak when Kåre spoke in a voice that surprised even him—a voice of maturity, a newfound wisdom, and authority, "I know this might be a lot to consider, but I agree with Asta. We all have thoughts, ideas, and adventures to have and establish. I have proven myself a worthy Viking and will ensure your daughter is safe. Mum and Dad, your son is now a man and will be a husband soon. You have taught me well, and I know being with Asta and helping her through her adventures will be an adventure of my own". Bjartr walked up with his soon-to-be wife and said, "We will go with you."

Though all the families involved were sad and worried, their eyes showed pride, which overshadowed any negative emotion. Balder put his hand on his wife's shoulder and spoke, "We must know this is not a loss but a show of the blood running through our veins. The Viking spirit of adventure and conquest is kindled in the next generation. We will have the best celebration of marriage and life, the greatest of all because our family, beliefs, and passion are being expanded to new lands and through new adventures".

Asta and Kåre bowed their heads at these words. Astrid came to Asta, kissed her on the forehead, touched her hair, and told her, "Become the woman I was too scared to become." Hugs, handshakes, and congratulations were coming from everywhere. The young girls ran up to Asta. She knelt, and they began to touch her hair and say things like,

"It's happening."

"Will you come back and tell us more stories?"

"Say 'hi' to the elves for me!"

Two days later, in front of their long-house, the ceremony was performed for the union of the two families. The weather seemed to honor this union as there were clear skies, and a nice cold breeze swayed the long lace veil over Asta's face. Both Balder and Astrid came up and lifted the veil off her face. Kåre moved closer, then they placed the veil over his head, and they had their first kiss. It was a simple kiss but full of love and passion. This kiss filled Kåre with a warmth that moved through his body, and then it all rushed to his head.

Laughs and cheers from the girls erupted. Gasps from adults and catcalls from the young men caused the kiss to cease. Asta saw what the commotion was all about. Kåre's hair was now blonde. They stood under the veil, blessed and chosen by the Valkyrie. They walked up the stairs to enter their longhouse. They opened the door and made their way to their first adventure. There was one final cheer from the crowd, and then they all headed over to the fire pit, where food and drinks awaited them to celebrate the union of the families. Cheers, jokes, and children playing filled the soundscape, making it feel warmer than the early winter wind blowing in from the North.

Alone in their longhouse, unbothered by
visitors but surrounded by gifts and lots
of food, Asta and Kåre lost sense of time.
Day in and day out, they grew closer
and more fond of each other. What once
felt like it would be a coffin now became
a chrysalis. Soon, Up-Helly-Aa came
and went. The cold weather subsided;
the snow melted away. The time came
to prepare for life away from everyone.
Crates, bags, barrels, and baskets filled
to the brim were hoisted onto the ship.
On the dock stood the three families
who shared their final farewells and conversations, trying to delay departure.

One by one, they boarded the ship.
Girls waved excitedly, friends wiped
away tears, and families held each other
tightly. The brave four looked out at
this scene and waved. The sound of the
whirling wind slowly became louder. It
was like the sound of hooves galloping
in a field. The louder and louder it grew,
the stronger the gallop became. The
Valkyrie came to send off the adventurers.

A strong gust of wind filled the sails, making it seem like the boat took a deep breath, and off they glided on smooth waters. Bjartr and Kåre took to tying sails and steering the ship. Asta looked at Bjartr's wife and saw her tear-stained cheeks, now rosy from the wind. Asta grabbed her hand and reassured her, "We are going to be fine. We are both smart and brave. We have amazing Viking husbands".

Bjartr's wife grabbed Asta's hand and looked at her, and with a smile on her face, she said, "I know; I just didn't think I would be the lucky one to get out first." They smiled and looked at the men working, tying, and steering. Then they made their way toward the ship's bow and saw a vastness that, until now, had only been imagined. Before them was their future, their adventure. The world awaited their arrival, and they were ready for the world.

TALE 3
DARK VEIL: SAYO

The early sun's glow peered over the horizon. The welcomed warmth, carried by the breeze, flooded the ancient city as tradesmen and merchants began to leave their homes. A new day created opportunities to barter, haggle, sell, and profit. Everything appeared normal: the roads sparkled with dew, the Shogun's army stood like statues on guard, and the sound of children playing grew louder in the morning air.

Yet the Shogun's fear was given a voice at the city's southern end. In the presence of his officials and advisors, he decreed that starting that day, each family was only allowed to have one daughter. If a family had a second daughter, she would either be sold as a slave or killed upon discovery. This abrupt decree was fanned into existence by the fear of possible invasions by barbarians. The Shogun believed his city was unbalanced; there were fewer men than women, and a city could not defend itself without more men.

Blinded by irrationality, the Shogun became the thing he hated the most, the thing he swore he would fight against—a barbarian. Clouded by a shroud of worry, the Shogun's thoughts permeated the minds of his warriors and guards like poison, erasing emotion to the point of death. With these thoughts, the Shogun made it clear: any family with a second daughter up to the age of seven would be killed, and any daughter older than eight would be sold to foreigners as a slave. Publications of this decree was placed on every wall of the city, on every door of every house. These signs hung as ominous warnings, for they also read, "Raids will be executed upon the Shogun's request." These raids would occur until the Shogun believed a better balance was achieved.

Many people did not know what to expect; some were fearful and planned to leave the city, but were denied travel. Soldiers walked the streets. Their steps around the town taunted the inhabitants. The constant interruption of passing guards stifled the usual busyness of the market. The remainder of the day seemed longer and quieter, and hope waned. Though the feeling of a possible raid lingered in the city like a breath on one's neck. Night approached, bringing a sense of peace and in their homes, no one had to witness the encircling captors.

The moon was high in the cloudless sky. A gentle, cool breeze moved through the city, attempting to push away the day's despair. The yellow and black flags, honoring the Shogun, swayed atop the city walls. The gleam of the moon kissed every path, street, and wall. Then, a sound shattering the peace like glass filled the streets. A mother screamed as her nine-year-old daughter was taken from her home and dragged back toward the south end of the city. Another shouted and tried to fight off the guards as her three-year-old daughter was lifted by her leg and thrown into a large, horse-drawn wooden basin surrounded by samurai. Shouts and poundings awakened the city. The blazing fire of angered torches interrupted the moon's soft glow. The screams and shouts intensified the flames, fueling the fire with despair and sorrow.

At the other end of the city, by the western wall, Hideo and his wife Katsumi ran to the city garden with their child in hand. They avoided the guards at the gates and tried to make the least amount of noise possible. They weaved their way into the dense garden. Under any other circumstance, the lushness and beauty of this garden warranted a description. Yet, during this monstrous time and in respect of the innocence of the victims, the details will be overlooked.

Hideo and Katsumi entered the garden and placed their twelve-year-old daughter in the middle of the trees and shrubs. With tears in their eyes, they hugged their frightened daughter and told her to stay hidden until the noise stopped, and they returned to get her. With one last sigh, Hideo and Katsumi placed their hands on their child's head and prayed.

"May our love for you protect you from harm and strengthen you to face the path ahead. May it hide you from your enemies and serve as a sign of your courage. We love you, Sayo."

With that, they left her alone as the samurai approached closer and closer. Her shoulder-length white hair was a beacon that welcomed fate with open arms. The horses' steps became louder. Sayo, scared and nervous, began to cry. Tears filled and poured out of her eyes, yet she didn't make a sound. The samurai stopped right in front of her. The light from the torches lit up the garden. Sayo covered her face with her shaking hands. Torchlight moved from left to right, growling in search of prey. A few seconds later, which seemed like an eternity, the samurai continued on, to find their next victims. This surprised Sayo. She wondered why they hadn't seen her and just walked away.

The hellish night's noises slowly faded, and the moon's glow again filled the streets. In vain, it tried to bring back the stillness before the raid. Cries from families throughout the city filled the night air like a lament. Sayo lay down next to a boxwood shrub. She put her hands over her ears and fell asleep, still, with tears rolling down her cheeks.

Katsumi headed to the garden the following day, hoping Sayo would still be there. Step by step, she grew closer to the spot where she left Sayo the night before. Her eyes moved faster than her feet, but Sayo wasn't there. A sinking feeling hit her stomach so hard that it made her lose her balance, and she stumbled a bit. Frantically, covertly, she combed the garden, from shrub to shrub and tree to tree, the panic growing. Katsumi returned to where they had left Sayo the previous night; she sat there and began to cry.

The weight of the pain anchored her to the ground. Then, next to her, she noticed movement. Scared, she leaned away and saw a foot, then a leg. Still frightened, she reached toward the little barefoot, and at her touch, Sayo awoke and stood up. Katsumi was speechless. She reached out to touch Sayo's hair, which was now waist-length and black like the night sky. Katsumi hugged her daughter and asked her what had happened. A bit confused by her mother's voice, Sayo told her the samurai came close and left as if no one was before them. Katsumi, with delight, began to show Sayo her new and mysterious hair. Taken aback, Sayo started to cry. Katsumi held her close and told her, "You have truly been blessed, and this hair will speak of a new era; you will lead people of valor and courage, being able to conceal yourself from enemies in the night."

After a few more moments and hugs later, Katsumi told Sayo to stay in the garden during the day and at night, if possible, "come to the house." Katsumi kissed Sayo on the head, ran her hand through her hair, and once again left Sayo behind the veil of her black hair. During the day, Sayo stayed in the garden, while at night, she went to her house. The few precious hours she had of darkness were spent with her family, who were continuously amazed by the color of her hair and the strength and courage that seemed to be growing in her day by day.

Being unable to leave the garden during the day and with little to do, Sayo watched the samurai who trained in the courtyard about fifty feet away from the garden. Sayo would hide behind the shrubs and trees to look between the two stone walls, which had a gap about ten feet wide. Those ten feet were enough for Sayo to witness recruits being challenged, veterans being tested, and generals reminding everyone why they were generals.

Every day, Sayo observed and memorized everything during training. Once the session ended, she would head to the garden, stand on a stone slab, and replicate what she had learned. It didn't take long for Sayo to reach a point where she could confidently challenge recruits, and even some experienced warriors, and hold her ground. Though for the moment, her weapons were just branches and twigs, she wielded them with grace and confidence. As time passed, the garden that was her hiding place became her training ground. Days didn't seem as lonely as they turned into weeks. Weeks of progression. Weeks of strengthening.

One night, on a visit home, Hideo noticed this new strength in Sayo. Even at the young age of thirteen, Hideo knew his daughter was meant for greatness. That night, Hideo told Sayo something neither Sayo nor Katsumi had expected. Hideo cleared his throat and spoke, "At your young age, you have already grown to be a strong and courageous woman. This city is not ready for a great woman like you, but I know outside these walls, you can blossom into the beautiful woman you are meant to become. Instead of returning to the garden tonight, leave this place and create the future the night blessed you to have."

Katsumi stayed quiet, knowing this day would come, but never this soon. Sayo, encouraged by her father's words, which only confirmed what she was already thinking, stood up and hugged her parents. In that embrace, Sayo whispered to them, "I will be back, and I will hug you again, except in a better life and better circumstances."

Before Sayo left the house, her mom gave her a bag with bread, a small pot of cooked rice, and a few momos. Katsumi kissed her one last time. Her dad entered the kitchen from the bedroom carrying a dark green katana bag embroidered with purple, gold, and white Komainu. Sayo had never seen this katana before. Hideo approached Sayo and handed her the bag. "This was my father's; he was a great samurai, honored by the Shogun. I know it will serve you well, and you will use it for honor and justice." Sayo's face couldn't hide her excitement. She clutched the katana bag close to her heart, hugged her father, and disappeared into the night.

Her long black hair quickly hid her in the darkness; her feet didn't make a sound when she stepped. She was like a wisp of dark smoke in the night, unseen and unheard. She passed the garden and then walked through the open wooden doors of the city gate, which gave a clear view of the world beyond the city walls. Without any challenges, Sayo slipped through the guards and was now in the clear to continue her journey unhindered. In the dark, Sayo felt safe and protected. Walking wasn't tiresome because her excitement and nerves pushed her toward the unknown.

The night went by too quickly. As the first signs of light peered over the horizon, Sayo found a place to sit and rest before her first day of solar freedom. Though nervous, the reality of adventure and freedom drowned out her fears. She knew the love of her parents, which had to this day, kept her safe, would continue to do so. Sayo took a piece of bread in her hand and raised it to her face. She could smell family, love, and safety. There, in the hull of her family's love and the idea of a new life she could control, she stood up and moved toward the village at the edge of a small mountain that stood by a bamboo forest. She was now a day closer to her new beginning.

The road was lonely. Parts of it seemed unused, hidden by overgrown weeds and grass. As Sayo walked, her steps marked the path as her feet pressed grass and reed underfoot. The sun rose higher and higher. Not being accustomed to the direct sunlight with her black hair, she stopped a few times to avoid exhausting herself because she didn't know what the road ahead might present.

After midday, Sayo stood motionless in a field of tall grass. She heard rustling, the sound of someone else also walking through the field. Slowly, Sayo took her splendid green katana in her hand as her eyes scanned the brush. In a very happenstance manner, a young man eating a momo walked through the grass and passed in front of Sayo as if no one stood next to him. Sayo, shocked, followed the young man. Only a few steps into the chase, he turned around, mid-bite, and locked eyes with Sayo as the momo dropped out of his mouth.

He didn't speak or move. He was confused yet intrigued by what he saw. As the juice from the momo dribbled down his chin, Sayo mustered up the courage to speak,

"Hi."

The young man didn't speak. Sayo couldn't help but stare at his amber eyes and the beauty mark that decorated his left eye. Sayo tried again because she wanted a response,

"My name is Sayo."

"Uh-huh," said the now stunned young man. Sayo turned away slowly and continued her journey because no other words seemed to emerge from his mouth. After several awkward steps forward, Sayo turned around and saw the young man still there, like an extremely short, lifeless scarecrow. Sayo, unsure of what to make of the situation, continued her journey and pushed the experience out of her mind.

She continued her course through the grass field and several small hills. Drops of sweat began to roll down her forehead. Not a moment too late, a cool breeze swayed the grass and quenched the drops. After another hour of walking, Sayo stopped and sat by a small pond.

The sunset mesmerized Sayo. The colors mixed and blended in a beautiful dance of brush strokes to create the sky. The stillness of the pond, the softness of the grass, and the gentleness of the breeze made it easy for Sayo to decide to stay there for the night. Already, the fear of the shogun seemed distant and like another lifetime. Being hidden, sneaking around, and the sense of uncertainty were no longer at the forefront of her mind.

The sun hid under the horizon, allowing the stars' light to begin their display. Sayo lay on the lush grass, looked up at the stars, and breathed in the calmness and peace of the night. She knew she didn't have to worry about being seen because her black veil hid her in the darkness.

Sleep came quickly, and as it came, it left. Sayo opened her eyes. Slight glimmers from the stars were still visible but quickly waned as they gave way to the hazy light from the sun. Sayo washed her face with the cool water from the pond. She took out her last momo, looked at it, and smiled. The sweet smell of it reminded her of the mute dwarf scarecrow.

I don't even know his name.

After she laughed for a bit, she ate her momo, stood up, and went to the village just past this last hill. Through the fog, the glimmer of twilight was seen. The green wall of bamboo became clearer and nearer.

Every step brought her closer, making everything less hazy. There before her, the bamboo stood solid and unmoved. Sayo looked from left to right and then back from where she came, which was now blurred by the dissipating fog. She took a deep breath and walked into the forest of a new life, a new image, and a new worth.

After she walked for several minutes

through the dense forest, a sound began to fill the air. This sound was like a
distant memory, almost unrecognizable,
of children running and playing. She began to think about what she should do:
should I walk up and introduce myself?
Should I wait a bit and see if they are
friendly? Either way, this has to happen.
Sayo decided to walk up and hope for
the best. She stepped into view among
the villagers. Soon, the noise quieted.
Only the sound of silence was felt all
around. Everyone, young and old, stood
and stared as they saw what seemed
like an apparition, an ancient spirit of
a strong and beautiful ancestor. Sayo's
hair lay flat on her cheeks as she lifted
her head. The villagers didn't turn away.
They were amazed at this young woman
with raven black hair.

Almost simultaneously, all the young
girls ran to her to touch the beauty
of this new experience. Through the
sounds of the giggles from the girls and
whispers of attraction from the boys, a
serene and wise voice was heard,

"Who are you? What's your name?"

This was the voice of Minuro, the leader and counselor of the village.

"My name is Sayo," she responded, "The daughter of Hideo and Katsumi. I am here because I ran away from the cruel burden of the Shogun". A moment of silence was broken only by more villagers approaching the newfound visitor.

"Hatred and fear take many forms; it is wise to flee until one is ready to face and defeat them," Minuro continued. "You can stay here if you want, as long as you need, for you will know what you must do in time."

"Thank you..."

"Minuro."

"Thank you, Minuro," Sayo replied with a smile. The young girls flooded her with questions as the boys slowly got the courage to get closer. Sayo walked around and looked at all the pit houses. It was a strange feeling; she felt as if she knew what to expect, but then it was nothing as expected. This feeling confirmed what she knew, she had found a new home.

The continued admiration from both young and old helped break the ice. Conversations became friendships, and friendships became partnerships. The story of Sayo's time under the Shogun's power was asked to be repeated. A favorite among the villagers was the night Sayo received her black hair. Unable to describe the feeling of receiving the hair color because there wasn't a significant surge of power or a dramatic salutation from an ancient spirit, Sayo repeated the words her mom spoke over her and the calm she felt afterward, even when she was face-to-face with a soldier. All Sayo described was the reality of her gift; though it stemmed from the words of a mother, it was solidified in her training and belief in the injustice against young girls. Sayo began to share that this could happen to anyone who believed as she did and was willing to help others who were less fortunate and in need. The girls and boys began to ask to be trained. They all wanted to be a part of what they called the Shozoku Sayo. Boys, girls, men, and women who also felt the pain of injustice stood with Sayo, hoping to cause change, defend their rights, and protect their families.

Day after day, week after week, young and old came to be trained in the art of hand-to-hand combat and weaponry. Just as their passion grew, so did the black strands in their hair. One evening during training, the group went over stances and defense tactics. In unison, as if connected by a single movement, a perfectly orchestrated piece, the group of forty-nine warriors turned to the left in their ready position. At that moment, everyone noticed something moving around in the bamboo forest. No one moved; no one made a sound. All their eyes were fixed on the last point of inter-ruption.

Sayo, with her sword in hand, walked toward the forest. Closely behind her followed Shinkō, Nozomu, and Ai, her top students, now leaders in the Sho-zoku Sayo. Sayo raised her sword, and simultaneously, seamlessly, Shinkō, Nozomu, and Ai moved into the attack position. "We will not hurt you if you show yourself. If we have to find you, I can't make any promises", Sayo said in a smooth and confident voice. Even the wind seemed to hear the warning as complete stillness paralyzed the bamboo shoots. The two seconds of silence seemed longer because of the motionless surroundings.

Suddenly, two hands appeared stretched around a grouping of bamboo. First, hands, then arms, and finally, a head were seen. Sayo recognized the face despite lacking the momo dribble on its chin. It was the boy from the grass field. Sayo motioned for her fighters to back down. The boy approached almost as if he were in trouble. His hands were down to his sides, moving and flailing like deflated balloons, and his head bowed low. He would only move his eyes to look up at his reason for intruding: Sayo.

The boy began to speak. "Hi, my name is Nobu. I followed you here when we first met...well, when you first talked to me. I wanted to talk to you, but I was scared. I have been watching you train these people, and I wanted to know if you can also train me". Sayo looked at him, tried not to smile, and said, "Ok, you can train with us, but you must know you have a lot of catching up to do. Are you up for the challenge?"

"Yes, I am," Nobu replied excitedly, almost even before Sayo could finish her question. As his blushing subsided, they walked back toward the others, who had been in the same stance they were in since the interruption. When Sayo was close to the group, she motioned with her hand, and all at once, as if machines were powered down, their bodies performed synchronized movements to say thank you, and our work was done. With focus and intensity waning from their eyes, they made their way to greet the newcomer, who was standing clumsily close to Sayo. Questions about Sayo and Nobu's first meeting were inevitable. After Nobu told his side of the story, veering slightly from the truth, Sayo corrected the narrative, which caused some to laugh and others to put their hand on their mouth in shock and embarrassment for Nobu.

During the next training day, spotting the novice was easy. Not only because he didn't know or couldn't do most of the stances, but also because he was the only one among the warriors with entirely white hair; everyone had some black hair. Some had more strands than others, but they all had some black hair. Day after day, mishap after mishap, Nobu tried his best to learn and keep up with the Shozoku Sayo. This determination brought a smile to Sayo's face, and Nobu's affection for her began to be mirrored. When others enjoyed dinner or playing a game with friends, Nobu would practice his stances and weapons.

One day, after much hard work, Nobu was asked to come and demonstrate everything he had learned. Nervously, he approached the front of the statuesque group, turned and faced Sayo, bowed, and waited for her to begin to dictate the stances he must take. To his surprise, she bowed to him and then moved into an attack position. At the same time, the Shozoku Sayo moved to their at-ease position and then sat on the floor. All eyes were fixed on the student and teacher.

Nobu's eyes looked nervously in every direction. He swallowed hard. In the silence, Sayo moved to attack Nobu. With his eyes closed, Nobu let his muscle memory do the work. When he opened his eyes, Sayo stood behind him, ready for the next attack. He turned around awkwardly to prepare himself. The Shozoku Sayo released a percussive "Hai" to reset the spar. Nobu was ready. This time, he was determined to keep his eyes open.

She attacked again. Strike after strike, Nobu defended himself well. Block after block, Nobu held his ground. Then, what seemed out of thin air, Sayo brandished her sword. His nerves were visible by the drops of sweat on his forehead. He looked around for help because Nobu felt he would be defeated. Then, Minuro threw Nobu a naginata, and the percussion again sounded, "Hai!" The intensity in their eyes was palpable. Even the wind stood still to watch. Nobu breathed in deeply and attacked first. Clang, thump, "Hai".

The beautiful dance between the weapon and the wielder caused the Shozoku Sayo to stand on their feet in excitement. "Hai, Hai". The shouts became more frequent. Attack, defense, block, strike. "Hai, Hai, Hai". Spinning. Jumping. Crouching. Extending. Clang. Thump. Attack. "Hai". Movement after movement, you could see that Nobu's courage and strength began to grow. Turn. Jump. Block. Attack. Turn. Strike. Suddenly, Sayo paused.

Something made her lose focus. The onlookers gasped altogether. The Shozoku Sayo erupted in cheers. Nobu was confused and looked around frantically, then back at Sayo. She walked up to him and hugged him. Still dazed and confused, Nobu asked Sayo what had happened. With a smile, she put her hand on his head, removed his hair tie, and showed him his trophy. A black streak had appeared. Nobu grabbed his hair. Tears filled his eyes. Sayo placed her hand on his face and said, "Welcome to the Shozoku Sayo." Everyone ran up to congratulate Nobu.

The celebration continued all day and

into the night. The sounds of friendship and joy, which blended with the smells of great food, gave an instant jolt of happiness. Just like most gatherings, the people asked to hear the story of Sayo's journey to the village, but now, with the new portion of meeting Nobu. Late into the night, everyone celebrated their new warrior. As the moon began to disappear behind the bamboo and the night air became crisp, everyone headed to their own houses, full of food, happiness, and excitement.

The following day, everything seemed as usual. The sun brought in a warmth that pushed away the cold night air. The village dog began to make his rounds for his breakfast buffet. In her pit-house, already dressed and ready for the day, Sayo sat on her bed with her sword on her lap. She was pensive. These thoughts made her eyes seem distant and disconnected from her present. If you walked into her house, she wouldn't have noticed you, and you wouldn't believe she was there.

Her mind was full of questions about

what had to be done or whether she should do what she felt should be done. Her deep thoughts must have been projected beyond herself because Minuro entered as if invited. He sat on the floor and said nothing until Sayo realized he was there with her. A slight head turn in his direction, Sayo's mouth opened to speak, but the words seemed to be stolen by the questions racing through her head. Moving slowly, Sayo sat in front of Minuro.

"It's time I go and silence fear and injustice in my city," she said.

"Yes, it is time. It has been time for a while now, but it didn't matter until you recognized that your gift was given to you for more than just your protection. Now, go and protect the families and the city's future from the blind monster of fear", assured Minuro. Though earlier, the thoughts seemed to have clouded her mind and weighed her down, Minuro's words caused it all to evaporate. With a more confident nod, Sayo stood up, took a deep breath, grabbed her katana with her right hand,

and walked out to begin preparations.

 Sayo walked out of her pit house, looked around, and saw Shinkō, Nozomu, and Ai at the center of the village around a fire pit with embers fading away, giving their last flickers of celebration. In the middle of their conversation, the three stopped and looked toward Sayo, who now walked toward them and knew something was about to happen. Sayo stepped close to them and leaned in to speak, but Ai spoke, "We are ready," before she could say anything. That was all that needed to be said. They walked together to the training site and waited for the warriors to take their positions.

The Shozoku Sayo arrived in groups of five, then another three, then a group of seven, and then a few people came in by themselves, staggered by about three seconds each. They all took their places. Nobu ran in just in time to make it to his spot as Sayo began to speak.

"It is time for me to return home and de-fend the honor of the young women and the city. The manner of lifestyle imposed by the shogun is no life at all. I am ready now to face this monster and do what must be done to see the city free".

"Hai," they respond.

"I do not ask that you all join me in raising a new banner, but if you desire, you may."

"Hai", they roared again, but this time, it felt more like an agreement and contract than a response.

"We leave in an hour and will discuss tactics on the way. Take the weapon of your choice and food for two days. Join me here so we may leave promptly". Sayo didn't move from her spot. She had her sword and felt she didn't need to worry about getting food for the journey. Fifteen minutes later, Shinkō, Nozumu, and Ai arrived with their weapons and enough food for them and Sayo. All the Shozoku Sayo were present—one by one, each with their weapon and a small bag with their food. True to form, almost at the last minute, Nobu walked up with a weapon in hand and a bag

on his back with food that could feed
the entire group if he wanted. Sayo saw
him, smiled, and shook her head. Not in
disappointment, but rather in a way that
said, what could I have expected?

Without a word or a command, Sayo
led the way out of the village through
the bamboo forest. This time, the trip
through the forest was a bit different. It
felt like the feeling you get when heading
somewhere you don't want to be, but
must be there. Time went by fast and
slow at the same time.

Passing the bamboo forest, they made
their way toward a hill. Up the hill and
down the hill. Then they made their way
to the field with the tall grass, where
people began to ask,

"Was it here?"

"He didn't see you?"

"Why didn't you say anything?"

The day went on, and they were able
to make it to the pond where Sayo had

her rest on her previous journey. They decided to stay there for the remainder of the day. No words of strategy were spoken, just conversations between friends and laughter between loved ones. That night felt strangely peaceful and not heavy with the thought of battle. Nobu approached Sayo, seated by the pond with about six other people. He took random steps to the left and right, weaving between the group. He finally reached Sayo and sat next to her.

She noticed him and smiled at him. The other people in the group began to have their conversations and turned away from Sayo to give them privacy. Nobu leaned over and said, "I know this might be scary, but if anyone could do it, it's you." The admiration in his eyes was prevalent, and his words to Sayo felt warm as if she had just taken a sip of hot tea on a chilled evening. Sayo took her hand and grabbed Nobu's, lying on his lap. She gave it a gentle squeeze; his face turned slightly red. Nobu mustered up all his courage, lifted his hand with her hand still on it toward his lips, and gently kissed her hand. Sayo's smile made Nobu's heart skip a beat. He now felt ready to conquer the world.

After this, the others around them reinserted themselves into their conversation. After several jokes, talks, and teases later, people began to get tired and made their way to a spot in the meadow around the pond. As the light from the sun faded and the sound of crickets replaced the chirping birds, they began to fall asleep one by one.

Sayo lay there for a few minutes looking into the sky, not really thinking of anything, just looking; not looking for something, just looking. It felt strange to her that she would feel such a sense of peace before what she would do the next night, but she didn't question it. She allowed this feeling to continue, slowly closed her eyes, and fell asleep.

The following day, everyone got up at about the same time. Bags moving, weapons clanging, and water splashing added to the noise of birds chirping and the breeze blowing through the reeds. Everyone began their breakfast. They rekindled the fire to heat water for tea. It didn't take long before the sound of laughter and conversation began to build. It felt like a family camping trip, not a battalion at the brink of battle.

The morning was calm, and it quickly became noon. In the middle of all the conversations, Sayo stood up and directed herself to everyone, "We must plan our attack and prepare ourselves for what is to come." Everyone immediately organized their bags, grabbed their weapons, and sat in a perfectly spaced square before Sayo and her fierce three. "The best time to attack will be at night, as we will have the advantage of not only surprise but of our hair concealing us. Those with more white than black hair use the ashes from the fire to cover your hair. We will all enter through the front gate. There should be only six guards at the gate. Once they are taken out, we can prop the gate open to have enough room to let us get in. We don't want to alarm anyone to our presence by bursting through the doors. Once inside, I will need some of you to go around the city wall and eliminate any guards; we don't want anyone to make our presence known to the shogun. The rest of you will go through the city, ensuring no guards are on the streets. I will go with Shinkō, Nozumu, Ai, and Nobu to find the shogun to end his terror". Like a single drum hit, they all responded, "Hai."

"We will leave in two hours for our next stop and wait for nightfall there," Sayo continued. "We do this not out of anger or revenge but for justice and honor. I thank you for joining me. Soon, our family will grow, and we will be at peace again, Hai."

"Hai, Hai, Hai," the Shozoku Sayo's voices rang to confirm their commitment to the cause.

Dusk came very slowly. Now that tactics were planned and action would be taken, the air around the pond seemed thinner. Hearts beat a bit faster. Thoughts seemed to fly back toward the village past the bamboo forest, and emotions slowly drained energy from each of them. It wasn't until Sayo spoke and gave more instructions that they began to come back to their warrior state. They were instructed to cover any metal or reflective items with cloth and to change into their green samue for camouflage. After this, they made their way closer to the city.

Remaining still at a distance, they camped at the bottom of a hill about a mile from the gated city. Here, darkness came quickly, and spirits were high, ready for their mission. No moon rose in the sky, but the stars began to shine one by one like a cosmic crescendo of celestial light. The entire company walked to the top of the hill and lay on their stomachs, and they peered over to see the wall, gate, and the torches that blazed around the top perimeter of the wall. By the gate, no light signaled the beginning of curfew for the city.

"One more hour, then we will begin," said Sayo. These words were like a password to start an elaborate machine because the entire Shozoku was divided into squads or sections, and they began sharpening their weapons.

The time had finally come. Sayo stood with her chosen four, and everyone dispersed in different directions. Their feet didn't make a sound as they ran or, what seemed more like, gilded towards the walls and gate. The shining light from the stars helped guide the company through the unknown territory. If you were standing on the city wall looking out, it would have seemed motionless. A gentle breeze was giving the Shozoku Sayo a push toward their target.

The entire group reached the wall and stopped. Once they stopped, the breeze began to blow a little more consistently. The shogun's flags fluttered, and the torches roared. Four Shozoku slowly approached the gate and crouched low. They waited for their chance to strike quickly and quietly. Sayo would have been confused if she had not been privy to the plan because the guards by the gate fell to their doom from what seemed to be a clear mist or poisonous gas.

The front gate opened slowly with just enough space to squeeze inside. At this sight, the rest of the company made their way to the gate and entered as quickly as the soft glow of the torches' light poured inside. Sayo and the other four waited until they were all inside, and the guards on the top of the wall facing out from the gate were taken down. This was their signal to make their way in and toward the shogun's palace.

Sayo led the way. With their weapons out, they ran toward the gate. Ai went through it first to ensure the coast was clear for Sayo to enter. It was. They ran through the central street toward the middle of the city. Soundlessly, the Shozoku advanced their way around the top of the wall, eliminating every guard. The ground forces made light work of the unsuspecting guards. Sayo got closer and closer to the shogun's house. Laser focus began to fill her eyes. Then, like an alarm that starts one awake in the morning, a loud crash interrupted the progress.

They all stopped and looked back. Nabu had tripped and fallen into a basin that fell over and cracked in half. They stood motionless for a few seconds while more and more torchlight filled the streets. The general's shouts led to more guards flooding the city. The Shozoku Sayo went to the city streets to fight the newly aroused guards. Shouts, clanging, and crashing were heard throughout the streets. Sayo and her section continued their course toward the shogun.

They didn't encounter many guards, as most of the fighting was on the outer streets. Yet, when any guard confronted them, they took them down immediately. They ran around the city center court and up the last block of residential and market streets. Then, it all seemed quiet since the fighting was behind them in the lower quarters. Their run became a steady walk. In formation, they made their way up a narrow stone road flanked by two ponds. Then, the road was flanked by two grass patches. Then, the road became a path, and then it became a walkway.

Finally, they were standing in front of a shoin-zukuri mansion, the house of the shogun. The four guards at the door seemed no challenge as Nobu, Shinkō, Nozomu, and Ai took them down with just a few moves. Shinkō and Nozomu opened the doors as Nobu and Ai ensured the path was safe and clear for Sayo. In formation, they walked through the first two rooms into the great hall before turning left. There, they saw the shogun standing at a table, protected by five guards, standing before him with swords drawn.

Sayo walked confidently, directly toward the shogun, blind to the guards. She grew two steps closer, and the guards charged at the intruders. Even when they began to fight against the guards, Sayo's eyes never seemed to lose focus on her real target. Swords collided, and feet moved on the floors and walls as if no one obeyed gravity. If one were watching it, one would be enamored by the beauty of the synchronization of this fatal dance.

And like a dance, the unrehearsed began to get tired. The guards were slowly drained from the fierce battle. This show of weakness gave the

Shozoku Sayo the chance they needed
to overpower their opponent. Almost
at the same time, they defeated their
foe with different but powerful strikes.
One by one, the fallen bodies sank to the
ground. Sayo walked toward where her
eyes still looked intently. Once again,
they walked in formation.

Three steps away from the shogun,
Shinkō and Nozomu squatted down,
spun on their heels, and swept the back
of the shogun's knees, which caused him
to fall forward and land on the ground.
As the shogun tried to use his hands to
catch himself, Ai and Nobu flipped over
his exposed arms and tied a rope around
his wrists. When they landed, they
flipped over his body and twisted the
rope behind him. Shinkō and Nozomu
placed their feet on his knees as Nobu
and Ai pulled the rope tight to pull the
shogun's shoulders back. Then Shinkō
and Nozomu held his head up by grip-
ping his hair.

Breathing heavily, the shogun finally
looked at his attacker in her eyes. Step
by step, strength and confidence encour-

aged Sayo to speak. "You don't know me, but I have feared you for long enough. Now you must answer for the blood of all the young girls you despised, Osore". A smirk appeared on Osore's face, and he prepared to speak. A swift, concise SWOOSH was heard before he could utter a word. Osore, with his eyes wide open, felt his life leave his body through the slit across his throat. Sayo's sword reflected the glow of the torches as crimson pearls of victory dripped on the wooden floor. Osore was no more. His body collapsed to the ground. With tears filling her eyes, Sayo turned around and walked away from Osore; the Shozoku Sayo followed suit.

When they walked outside, they noticed people filling the streets. The towns-people were confused not only about the guards who lay dead on the roads but also about the black-haired invad-ers. Not knowing whether to celebrate or be afraid, everyone was silent. Sayo kept walking, paying little attention to her surroundings. All she wanted was to get to her house and see her family. She didn't have to go very far, as her parents were among the ones investigating the newcomers. Sayo was about twenty steps from her parents when they stopped and slowly turned around as if they knew Sayo was approaching. When they turned, they saw Sayo walking toward them and began crying. This cry was not of sadness but pride, relief, and joy. They both hugged Sayo, and Sayo knew she was finally back home.

The next few days were spent retelling the story told to the Shozoku Sayo. In these retellings, Nobu was mentioned. Both men and women, young and old, wanted to be trained and join the ranks of the Shozoku Sayo. It wasn't long until the townspeople asked Sayo to be their shogun, the first woman leader. Sayo was honored and accepted the position. White flags with black Yatagarasu replaced the black and yellow flags of Osore. Along the side with the poles, these flags boasted a golden braided rope with tassels on both top and bottom. A thinner, golden, braided rope aligned the edges on the other three sides of the flag. The black Yatagarasu was embroidered along the edges with blue, crimson, and violet thread. These flags heralded something new, something of renown. This era of freedom and unity paved the way for exciting experiences. More and more, it became natural to have black hair. Soon, all the townspeople were either fully black-haired or, at the least, in the clan of Nobu, with just a streak of black.

TALE 4
WILLOW: ALDRICH

Perukes are a type of wig. That is how it is taught in history classes. The reality was that people were so proud of their white hair that they began to style it, add powder, and even scented ointments. Nowadays, perukes are used as a traditional nod to this time, as if one wants to remember the English people's rigid, superficial way of life. There were hopes and glimmers of progress with Mozart, Charlotte Turner Smith, and Joshua Reynolds, but the aristocracy's reins demanded order and tradition. Usually, such tight reins produce more creativity and freedom in an artist's mind. But to a boy becoming a man, what would that expression be? You might ask, "What does this have to do with the story, or when does the story begin?" This has

everything to do with the story that
starts now.

Aldrich sat at his desk, which faced a
sizable second-floor window. This view
showed a large estate garden with a not-
so-subdued water fountain at the center.
Beyond the garden was a large grassy
field that sloped downward towards
a river that served as a border to the
untamed woods. In the garden, he saw
his mother in her sacque dress as she
directed the servants on what to do for
the evening dinner guests.

Aldrich just sat there, not writing
or moving much. He just sat, lost in
thought. In front of him, on the desk, lay
a stack of papers containing a speech his
father had prepared for him to recite at
the dinner party. This was a coming-of-
age dinner for him. What does it even
mean, he thought to himself. What is
this all for? Does it mean my thoughts
until now were futile and meaningless
without clout or dignity? Aldrich again
questioned the structures and formali-
ties of life. He reasoned that if they were
so important, why was this only offered

to the gentry and nobility, not the workers, artists, musicians, scholars, writers, or adventurers? At this time, these occupations were looked down upon and seen only as jobs for hire, as pomp for the pleasure of the aristocracy. Even the crown glorified itself in the luxury of others' hard work, claimed it as its own, and paid pennies as hush money.

The dinner that night proved this obstinate thought: lavish food, friends in high places, servants in theirs, rubbing elbows for self-gain, and a speech of matching plumage with the most prideful peacock. Of course, to others, this speech and the extravagance of everything else seemed as expected as the sun's rising. But unlike the sunrise, this decadence didn't give Aldrich the same feeling as when the early sunlight flooded through his window every morning. The sunlight beckoned him, calling him to be more and different, just like every sunrise.

There, as he sat at the desk, his mind raced. His hair lay on his face on either side of his eyes, down to his cheekbones, while the rest of his hair in layers went down to his shoulders. Brown eyes stared into the ebbing light of the early evening. His left hand grabbed the stack of papers in front of him and flipped them over. There was a knock at the door.

"Sir, your mother wanted me to make sure you had what you needed for dinner," said a voice from the other side. This voice belonged to the estate's butler and Aldrich's closest friend, Harvey. Harvey was an accomplice to Aldrich's crazy ideas of a free world. His ideas contained a reasonable amount of different, traditional, or better yet, a mixture of the two.

Harvey didn't hear an answer from the young master, so he knocked again and slowly opened the door. He saw Aldrich sitting at his desk, barefoot, with his trousers and shirt on haphazardly. His dinner attire lay on the bed, untouched. Harvey walked toward Aldrich and stood to his right side, just out of sight.

"Everything ok, sir?" asked Harvey

almost in a whisper. Without changing expression or even glancing over, Aldrich responded, "All this for nothing. The food, music, and guests for a parade of nothing. What am I coming of age to? What is it I can finally do that I couldn't do before? It shouldn't be called coming of age but more like coming of blasé. But I guess now I have the right to barter my talents and wit for a position in society, to have my voice heard or, better yet, my pocket heard". Tears filled Aldrich's eyes, tears not of sadness but of frustration and realization.

Harvey placed his hand on Aldrich's shoulder, squeezed it slightly, returned it to his side, and awaited orders. "Thank you, Harvey," Aldrich said finally. "I will begin to get ready for dinner shortly. Tell Mom all is well and on schedule." Harvey gave a slight nod, turned around, walked out of the room, and closed the door behind him.

Still seated at his desk, Aldrich looked down at the notes, turned them right side-up, and glanced over them one last time. Frustrated, he stood up and grabbed the papers tightly in his hand. After a much-needed deep breath, he walked toward the fireplace. Aldrich stopped in front of the unlit hearth and threw the carefully crafted words of Hiram's discourse into the fireplace to be the perfect kindling for his fire. Aldrich took the sulfur match, knelt, and ignited the papers. He stood up and walked away. He sauntered back toward his desk, put his hands on the chair back, and transferred his weight onto his left leg as he leaned over the chair.

He stared off into the now dusk sky. If his thoughts were given a sound, they would have drowned out the crackling paper in the fireplace. Aldrich took another deep breath and shook the chair left and right as a self-motivated pep rally. This was better than slapping himself because his face would have been too red. Prodding questions would dampen his mood even more than it had already presented itself. Wanting not to think about anything anymore, Aldrich walked toward the washroom. He splashed his face with water, dried his face with a rag, and then wiped the back of his neck.

He walked back to his bed, where his dark blue frock coat lay with its golden embroidery framing the lining, making a stately statement that gave the wearer instant status.

He grabbed the coat at the collar, turned it in his hand, and slung it behind him. The coat opened and landed perfectly on his shoulders, so all he had left was to slide his arms in and button up. As he was buttoning, there was another knock at the door. Before he could answer, the door swung open. It was his father, Hiram. Imagine Aldrich as someone who demanded attention in a room. Now, imagine a person who is more prominent and made more attractive by age.

As Hiram walked in, he glanced at the fireplace, "Hmm, a bit hot today for a fire, don't you think?" Aldrich looked over nervously to inspect the arson remains, but couldn't see any smoldering papers.

Trudy, the family foxhound, ran into the room as a welcome distraction. Her tail wagged excitedly, always making Aldrich smile, but constantly annoying Hiram. Trudy sat next to the bed, tongue out, and panted while she waited to witness the conversation. Still smiling from Trudy's arrival, Aldrich looked at Hiram and saw his dad's eyes bewildered by his still childish reaction to a dog.

"I see you're not ready yet. Guests will arrive within the hour, and I want you with me to greet them as they arrive".

"I'll be ready," replied Aldrich, and almost in between breaths, Hiram added, "I know you will be."

Hiram turned around, walked out of the room, and left the door open. It seemed he expected Trudy to follow and close the door for him. Trudy still sat in the same spot, with a dog smile on her face and her tail wagging back and forth, which made a thud sound on the Persian rug. Aldrich walked over to the sitting area by the fireplace, sat on one of the cushioned, armed chairs, and began to put on his buckle shoes. Trudy took this as an invitation to come over, and she began to lick his hands and ask for a pet. Aldrich chuckled, patted her on the head, and began to talk to her in a voice every dog owner recognized. Trudy's tail couldn't decide which direction to wag to express her excitement, so it looked like her tail was outlining a large circle.

Aldrich couldn't remember when he felt sad while with Trudy. It was as if Trudy were happiness itself. So, wherever Trudy was, happiness was there as well. This seemed like a good change for Aldrich, for he knew in a few hours, he would become a man in the eyes of society. He must "make his father proud" and "keep respect for the family name."

After Trudy satisfied her dosage of attention, she just gave a small bark as if to say 'thank you' and trotted away. Once again, he was alone in his room, fully dressed and ready to face the aristocracy and their pointless expectations. He walked over to the window and looked down toward the garden courtyard, where some of the servants were already in their positions, and others began to light the candles. Aldrich fixed his coat, cleared his throat, and walked toward the door. On his way out, he grabbed his hat off the bed and put it under his left arm.

Passing down the hall with its wooden floor, all that could be heard was the sound of Aldrich's shoes, which made a tapping sound with every step that seemed to mimic the tick of a clock. He turned left and went down the staircase facing the front door. Through the glass, he could see a carriage had pulled up. At the bottom of the stairs, he did an about-face and headed toward the large French doors that led to the courtyard. Before he walked through the doors, he put on his hat and gave his coat one final tug.

If Aldrich hadn't been distracted by his thoughts, he would have enjoyed the splendid, yet excessive, setting. Candelabras lined the entire back of the house, adding a nice warm light to the stone walls and floors. Five round tables covered by crisp linen tablecloths with an embroidered, scalloped lace hem about ten inches wide were set to one side of the fountain. On each table was an assortment of pastries, fruits, cheeses, breads, cured meats, and olives. Men and women stood throughout the courtyard holding serving trays with glasses of champagne. A large wooden table stood on the farthest side of the courtyard, close to the grassy field. As if the flowers from the planters on the courtyard corners weren't enough, the center of the entire table was lined with an array of greenery, flowers, vases, and candles. Elaborate place settings with beautiful cloth place mats for each guest gave the final touch of class.

Aldrich made his way to stand next to his father. His father examined him and gave him a nod of final approval as the first guests walked in. A couple, known more for Lady Margaret than Sir what's-his-name: for he married above his station, and luckily for him, Lady Margaret could maintain and increase her father's wealth. Of course, doing the work under her husband's name. Hiram and Aldrich bowed, kissed her hand, and welcomed her as Aldrich's mom walked her to her seat, admiring the flowers and decorations. Sir what's-his-name walked up, and Aldrich extended his hand for a handshake. Confused, as this was a new practice, Sir what's-his-name just grabbed his hat and tipped it slightly. Hiram did the same.

Hiram looked at Aldrich and forced a smile, "What was that? Were you going to kiss his hand, too?"

"No, I was going to shake his hand; it's a way of greeting someone," Aldrich replied. "Maybe if you're in a pub, but not here," hissed Hiram between gritted teeth and his fake smile. Before Aldrich could retort, the doors opened, and in walked Lord Harrington and Lady Marie, the owners of most of the cargo ships and ports in England. Whatever one might picture, they resemble the opposite. Both were very attractive and seemed too sweet to be such power-ful negotiators and the first people to almost form a monopoly in shipping cargo. Their shrewd business practices walked the line of legality, though they never broke the law. As for fortune, they were the wealthiest guests of the night, but their personalities always made one feel welcome and equal.

As they walked in, Lady Marie bowed toward Aldrich and Hiram, then swiftly walked over to Lady Margaret and Aldrich's mom. Based on the chatter, it appeared as if they hadn't seen each other in months, but they were just at high tea a couple of weeks ago. Lord Harrington tipped his hat, walked up to Sir what's-his-name, and began to entertain his idle prattle. Then in walked the Whitbreads, who had the brewing dynasty, then the Smiths, who were bankers, and lastly, the Strutts, who were the textile monarchs. Finally, with them came everyone's children—well, their older boys. A couple already had the pleasure of coming of age, and the others were soon to do so, along with three of the sisters who were ready to find a match out of these lucky gentlemen.

Aldrich took this chance, walked away from his father, and sidled to the boys already standing by the table, trying to figure out who would sit next to which sister. As Aldrich walked up, he heard the tail end of a conversation.

"No, but then it leaves me to sit next to my sister," said the Smith boy.

"Oh, hey, Aldrich. Can you believe now it's your turn? You just came to mine last month," the Strutts boy excitedly stated.

"Don't make him nervous; he already doesn't want to do this," the Whitbread boy warned.

"Don't worry yourself; he will do fine," responded the Whitbread girl, whose piercing blue eyes always made Aldrich's heart skip a beat. Aldrich turned and looked at her, and once again, because this happened every time he saw her, it was like he lost his footing and caught himself. "Well, I guess it's settled. Aldrich will sit between me and my sister", said the Whitbread boy with a slight grin. Aldrich moved quickly to hide his blushing face by going to her seat. He pulled out the chair and tipped his hat before he sat between the Whitbread's legacy.

Dinner and drinks mixed in, as did the

conversations everyone was engaged in. The latest news of the shipments from Spain, the newest textiles imported from India, and thoughts of opening new banks in other towns made Aldrich's conversation with his friends seem juvenile and inconsequential.

"When can we go back and swim at the lake?" asked Philip, the Strutts boy.

"We don't have much time as it is going to start to get cold soon," remarked James, the Whitbread boy.

"So let's go in two days, and we can stay over the weekend. My parents just had the house cleaned, and they won't be returning until next spring", said Hugh in a matter-of-fact tone (the Smith boy). The servants removed the empty dinner plates and cups from the table. All the boys took this as a sign to move chairs around the table to aid their conversation about weekend planning. The girls stood up and walked to the pastry and fruit table, as the conversation didn't require their participation.

Aldrich's face fell as realization again threw adult life into his plans. All the boys looked over at him because he wasn't participating in the excitement. "I'll have to start work with Dad," he said. "Yeah, but not for another week," replied James and continued, "This weekend can be the coming-of-age party for all of us. We can do what we want or do nothing. It would be up to us." "I'm going to be naked the entire time," said Hugh, which made the boys laugh. Jolted with a new sense of freedom, Aldrich rejoined the conversation. Plans were made official with handshakes all around.

Aldrich looked up toward the pastry table and caught Julia's eyes. They both stared at each other. Julia stared more naturally than Aldrich, as his mouth was open, and he stared blankly. "Go talk to her," Philip nudged. Aldrich's head nodded, but his body didn't move. Phillip chuckled, stood up, and pulled Aldrich off the chair. Aldrich stepped slowly toward Julia, who smiled because she witnessed the ordeal.

As Aldrich approached her, he opened his mouth to speak, but he noticed that Julia's eyes looked to his right, and her smile faded. Aldrich looked over his shoulder and saw his father standing next to him. "Ready?" asked Hiram more as a formality, but he turned to address the guests without receiving a response. Aldrich stole one more glance at Julia. They both smiled, and Hiram began his discourse.

"Ladies and gentlemen, on behalf of my beautiful wife and myself, I would like to thank you for joining us in celebrating my son and the family's heritage. Soon, he will be joining me in revolutionizing carriage design and manufacturing. But first, he would like to share a few words."

Aldrich walked toward the fountain. The guests turned to face him. A couple of men held their walking canes firmly in their right hands. Hiram looked at Aldrich in surprise. He didn't have the speech he prepared in hand. Aldrich began, "Distinguished guests, admirable nobles, sirs, and madams." At this point,

Aldrich removed his hat. Everyone nodded in approval. "For quite some time, England has been built on the shoulders of great men and women like yourselves. The fruit of your purse has been seen not only by yourselves but by all in this room. Music, art, drama, and literature have blossomed under your watch. Your keen eye for proper critique and sensitive ears have marked the way to expression and creativity. London, no, England is established by the tastes of aristocratic desires. Europe looks to us as we look within for inspiration. Inspiration without a pocket is just a dream, but inspiration through a pocket is reality. Now, a question I pose to you. Are you to thank or to blame for our condition?".

Indignant confusion made its way across people's faces. Aldrich continued, "I will be happy to inform you that I will not be responsible for the stifling of artistic creativity nor the defilement of expression. I wish to be a worldly man who learned not of stock nor business but of life and experience. If God is the basis of all we do and He has created all we see, we would agree it is not traditional or monotonous. Then why are you, for I will not be?". Hiram's face turned stiff as shades of red flushed over it. A man stood up as he took umbrage at these remarks; the others hit the ground with their canes. Aldrich tried not to make eye contact. Both men and some women moved uncomfortably in their seats as if to find comfort for their pride.

"That is why, my brothers and sisters," Aldrich continued, "I fare thee well and bid thee adieu." At this, Aldrich took off his top coat. Some ladies looked away, and some men shouted through clenched teeth, "How dare you!" He threw his hat in the air and ran off through the tables, across the grassy field, and toward the river.

Hiram tried to reassure the indignant party that Aldrich wasn't feeling well. It might have been something he ate that made him speak so cheekily. "Bring out the whisky for these gentlemen and wine for the ladies," Hiram instructed Harvey, who stared out in the direction Aldrich ran with a smile. "Hear, hear," the in-jured parties replied. After a few throat clearings and coat tugs, the night music began to play once again. The aristocratic oblivion settled in like dew on a spring morning.

There, Aldrich stood on the banks of the river, his heart still beating fast, not because he had just run a good way but because years of thoughts and speech were finally released. What to do now? I should have run towards the road, not the woods, because I needed to figure out where to go. Aldrich looked back toward the house. He could see the glow of candlelight across the entire back of the house and barely make out the music being played. The music sounded like the music one might hear in a dream. One may know exactly what song it is, but when awakened, one can recall it, yet did not know which song it was.

He decided to walk to the right along the banks; if he hit a dead end or something else, he could retrace his steps to get back to this spot. Off he went. Realizing and remembering that this was only his second time being this close to the river, he slowed his pace. The other time he had been out here, he was about seven years old, and he had run away from home because his father wanted him to take oratory and Latin classes from a private tutor. Even from that age, Aldrich was very strong-willed and couldn't imagine having school after school. So, what comes naturally to a child is to run away. Once again, ten years later, he had done the same thing, but this time it felt justified. It's a bit un-planned and irrational, but justified. The more he walked, the less he could hear or see his house. In the moonlight, what he thought was a river now looked like a brook. He saw a spot where he could cross over.

As soon as he was on the other side, he began to hear Trudy's bark. It grew louder and louder, along with Harvey's voice encouraging Trudy to find Aldrich. He could have stayed there and returned to the house with them, but something in him convinced him to run. So he did. He ran smiling as if Trudy and Harvey were counting to one hundred, and he had to hide in the perfect spot to win the game.

Aldrich ran for about thirty seconds. He noticed a tree he could climb—up one branch, then another, then a third. In this tree, by this third branch, there seemed to be a hallowed spot big enough for him to hide. Aldrich climbed in, sat with his knees to his chest, wrapped his arms around them to bring his knees in as tight as possible, and leaned his head back onto the tree.

"Where is he, girl?" Harvey asked, a bit out of breath. Trudy walked around the base of the tree, where Aldrich hid, three times, then sat down and leaned on the trunk, tongue out and panting.

Harvey didn't look up but began speaking loud enough for Aldrich to hear. "Oh, Trudy, he got away from us. Hopefully, he is safe and knows what he is doing. If he had stayed longer, he would have heard his friends who agreed with him and convinced their parents not to take it personally. Also, after the initial shock, his mom and Lady Mary walked away from everyone, shared laughs about what happened, and even wished they had done the same when they were younger. The best part was when his dad apologized for what Aldrich had done. But to the surprise of those present, especially his mother, he said Aldrich would be the first in the family to have fun while he worked. To which the men, who were still slightly ticked, smiled and said things like 'Oh, to be young again.'"

Harvey bent down to pet Trudy, whose tongue was still out, trying to cool off, "I'm proud of you," he continued as if he were talking to Trudy, "But remember, if you leave again, make sure to take your clothes with you." Harvey placed Aldrich's overcoat on the closest branch. He kept his hand on it a bit longer, as if holding Aldrich's shoulder like he had done earlier that day in Aldrich's room. Harvey walked back toward the house, and with one whistle, Trudy looked up the tree, barked once, and followed Harvey.

With a smile, Aldrich climbed down the tree and grabbed his coat. He climbed back up and into the hollowed tree. Surprisingly comfortable, Aldrich leaned back and fell asleep in this old willow tree. The dream world welcomed Aldrich. In his dream, he swam in the lake with various carriages swooshing past him. Each had an emblem of his father's face, which asked him, "Ready?" Aldrich plunged himself underwater to escape the carriages. In the depths, he saw Julia with piercing blue eyes at the bottom of the lake. She sat surrounded by pastries, each of which seemed to smile at Aldrich.

Lower and lower, he swam to get closer. Julia's white hair swayed in the water, her eyes fixed on Aldrich's. Then her smile turned into a face of confusion. Aldrich floated in front of Julia, perplexed by her gaze, and asked, "What's wrong?" Julia responded, "It's your…" Julia extended her hand toward Aldrich's head. The dream stopped. The morning sunshine on Aldrich's face caused him to nictate, and the dawn beckoned him to emerge from his wooden cocoon.

Aldrich sat on the tree's exposed roots and considered what to do next. As he thought, he walked back toward the house. Why did I run away? I could have just recited my dad's speech. I could have talked with Julia. Julia. What did she want to tell me in my dream? He was back at the river. He crossed over and trekked up the hill toward the court-yard.

Trudy was running and barking at the birds that got too close to the fountain. As Aldrich approached, Trudy saw him and ran toward him, barking. She suddenly stopped. She sniffed the air in Aldrich's direction. Aldrich, confused by this, stopped and knelt.

"Come on, girl."

Trudy whimpered and apprehensively walked toward him with her tail down. When she was close enough, she sniffed his hands, then burst into jumps and tail wagging. Elation. The conversation between tail wagging and dog owner language was blissful.

"Trudy, come inside!" yelled Harvey. Trudy did not respond, so he walked into the courtyard and noticed the scene unfolding on the hillside. A bit more stern, Harvey yelled, "Trudy!" She licked Aldrich's face several times and headed to Harvey to tell him the news. Aldrich stood and walked toward the house. "Sir," Harvey said with confusion in his voice.

"Harvey, are you okay?" asked Aldrich.

"Sir, your hair," responded Harvey.

"I know I need to wash it; it's been a long night," stated Aldrich.

"No, sir. It is brown, but I don't think it's dirt," replied Harvey as he examined Aldrich's hair. The touch and feel were expected, but the color that Harvey thought was dirt wasn't coming out. So, he ushered Aldrich into the house and up to his room.

Everyone in the house stared at Aldrich, mouths opened, with a few double-takes. Aldrich entered his room and then went into the washroom. He looked in the mirror and wiped it as if there was something on it that kept him from seeing himself. No matter how much he wiped, his hair looked different. He poured water on his head and scrubbed it fiercely. He was sure the dirt would have washed off. To his surprise, the color remained. Was this what Julia was trying to tell him in his dream? My hair is brown. This is a different way to come of age. Why is my hair brown?

This was one of the most accidentally rebellious things he could have done. The only one with brown hair, and it happened right after the big speech. Whether Aldrich wanted to be or not, it didn't matter because now he would be seen as an insurgent. If his dad hadn't been angry with him last night, he might erupt when he sees this latest development. To draw out the inevitable, Aldrich decided to take a bath. As he sat in the water for a few minutes, the memory of his dream appeared. He thought: Even if I wanted to, I don't think Dad would like me to work with him with my hair like this. Being ready wasn't the issue now; desire wasn't the issue; what would Dad say and do when he saw me? I would immediately be made the family recluse.

"He is ill".

"He isn't himself", would be my parents' conversation or excuse.

The bedroom door opened, and Trudy trotted in before Harvey entered. Trudy sat herself at the entrance to the washroom because she knew she wasn't allowed to enter. Her head turned and looked toward Aldrich while her tail began its cadence on the wooden floor. Aldrich could not delay anymore, so he ended his bath. He stepped out of the tub and dried himself. Harvey's voice rang out from the room,

"Everything good, sir?"

"Yes, just finished bathing, now getting dressed," answered Aldrich.

With only trousers on, Aldrich walked into the bedroom. Trudy did not move from her spot at the threshold because she wanted a head pat as Aldrich walked by. Harvey stood by the desk, looking out the window now filled with sunshine. Harvey turned around and looked at Aldrich with a smile, and as he opened his mouth to speak, Hiram entered the room.

Both Aldrich and Harvey looked at Hiram and then at each other. Harvey excused himself from the room as Hiram walked to where Harvey was standing. Without acknowledging Aldrich's hair color, Hiram spoke, "Last night was interesting." Aldrich stood in one spot, trying not to make any movements so as not to cause his dad to turn and look at him. Hiram continued, "After your the-atrics, as you can imagine, your...friends began to laugh. I had to laugh to keep everyone from uncomfortably squirming in their seats. We all began to reminisce about our coming-of-age stories and thoughts of insurgency. Did you think that was the best way to get your point across?"

Aldrich stared at his father, still wonder-ing why he was talking about last night and not his hair. Hiram didn't wait for an answer. Instead, he continued, "This morning, I heard whispers from the staff, 'It happened to him too'". Aldrich's confusion became more pronounced on his face.

Before Hiram continued, Aldrich began to plead his case. "I feel like I am being forced into something I don't want. A job, no, a life I don't want." Aldrich looked at his dad, whose face was without reaction. Aldrich continued, "I want to feel like I haven't arrived. Like I am still moving and going forward. I'm not sure if I stay here, I can move forward". Hiram looked at Aldrich with a look Aldrich hadn't seen before and responded, "That is called striving, and it's what I have always wanted for myself and for you. It isn't that you don't achieve something, but it means you continuously achieve something". Aldrich's eyes filled with tears because his father had just put into words what he had been trying to define for the last three years, and he replied wholeheartedly, like a sigh of relief, "Yes."

Understanding and mutual ground were finally solidified between father and son. Aldrich never felt closer to his father than at this very moment. Before Aldrich could say something else, Hiram spoke, "I know the family business might not seem like an adventure or an endeavor you would want to join me in, but as long as you find something that keeps you striving for more and challenging, that is all I want." Aldrich never thought he would hear these words from his father. With this open invitation to leave his family legacy, Aldrich felt, much to his surprise, he would be content staying with his father as he, for the first time, saw his father with the same adventurous spirit he possessed.

Hiram walked toward Aldrich, put both hands on his shoulders, and said, "The real question is, what are we going to do and say about this hair?" They both smiled and walked toward the two chairs by the fireplace. Aldrich told his dad about his dream and the events of the previous night. This was the lengthiest conversation between the two, and at moments, you couldn't differentiate between father and son as they shared many of the same qualities and mannerisms. Trudy made her way to them and lay with her tongue out, on the floor in front of them. Her head went back and forth from father to son, like watching the tennis ball go back and forth from player to player. Happiness filled the room, not because Trudy was present, but because realization and understanding pushed away any fear and confusion. The two men shared meaningful moments of common ground.

A continuation of everyday life for Hiram was a fresh new look at life for Aldrich, but of course, it was not until after a trip to the lake house and a retelling of the night's happenings that it was. It wasn't clear whether or not people cared about Aldrich's hair being brown, but the more his relationship with his dad strengthened, the more he realized his dad also had brown hair. It contained more white than brown, but brown nonetheless. All this time, what Aldrich wanted to achieve and the life he wanted to live was being given to him by his father, who had already gone through this process with his father—a generational legacy at its finest.

Brown hair seemed the norm in the

house. As for most people outside the four walls, stares and questions were the usual. This didn't bother Aldrich because his dad beamed with pride over his son. Friends didn't care about his hair. The family supported his decisions. Aldrich felt supported and understood. His life felt like it was his own, moving to his rhythm. Now, on to his life's biggest challenge and adventure: Julia.

TALE 5
BLACK CROWN: TLACELEL

The air was calm, and the entire forest was silent. Tlacelel's gaze was locked onto a specific point. While one's eyes could only see a group of trees and shrubs, he observed a black and brown rabbit enjoying a meal of green zinnia leaves. Oblivious to the hunter, the rabbit continued to munch while the hunter prepared to use his sling swiftly.

Tlacelel's right hand shot back in a split second, made a small whip forward, and released one side of the sling. The small rock darted through the brush, leaving a hole through all the green foliage, drawing a line straight to the rabbit's head. CRACK! The rabbit turned over twice from the impact. It happened so quickly that it appeared to be chewing for a moment, and then suddenly, it was lifeless. The young man walked over to his fresh kill.

He attached his sling to his maxtlatl and lifted the game by its hind legs, holding it up high. About ten warriors cheered, "Ja!" before approaching him to offer congratulations. Tlacelel was the sole member of the royal family related to Emperor Milintica, who engaged in hunting for their sustenance. Amid conversations, a young servant approached Tlacelel, took the rabbit, and placed it around his neck. Together, they all turned and headed back towards the city.

A magnificent scene unfolded as the dense forest and bushes gave way to a sight that rivaled European buildings and the Egyptian pyramids. The trees abruptly stopped, revealing a vast expanse of vibrant green grass stretching around the lake as far as one could see. At the heart of the expansive lake stood the majestic city of Tenochtitlan.

Crossing the bridge into the city's outskirts filled every individual with pride. The royalty, commoners, and laborers admired the bridges, streets, houses, temples, and palaces. The city appeared more advanced than even London or Madrid, thanks to its cleanliness, maintained by the sophisticated water systems they had established. In the radiant morning sun, the prince and his entourage journeyed towards the palace in the eastern part of the island.

Tlacelel strolled through the palace courtyard, ascended the stairs to the landing, circled the second-floor terrace, and climbed another set of stairs to reach the rooftop tub supplied with water from the nearby mountain springs. Entering the bath, the cold water immediately revitalized his body. He splashed water on his face, ran his fingers through his hair, and stood at the tub's edge, gazing at the mountains and forest.

While lost in contemplation, envisioning the remarkable sight of an eagle landing on a cactus with a serpent in its mouth, a sudden flash of light snapped him back to reality. Scanning the surroundings in search of the light's source, he found nothing unusual along the banks and the tree line. Taking one final dive into the water, he emerged before stepping onto the rooftop.

The day's warmth quickly dried him off as he donned his tilmàtli and went to the courtyard, where he knew everyone would be gathered, eagerly awaiting his arrival. Upon entering, Tlacalel scanned the courtyard. His family sat quietly at the table. Drapes hung overhead, casting gentle shade from one side to the other in an intricately woven design. The courtyard's edges were adorned with honeysuckles, marigolds, and passion flowers, while clusters of cacti stood tall at each corner, exuding a captivating strength. The stone columns sparkled with hints of gold.

Tlacelel sat down at the table, and as the food was served, all the guests, including Milintica, took some of the maize porridge with honey and sprinkled it on the ground. Following Milintica's lead, everyone began their meal. The courtyard soon echoed with lively dialogue,

jokes, and stories once Milintica initiated conversation. During the morning
feast featuring tortillas, beans, and
vegetable sauce, congratulatory smiles
and nods were exchanged towards
Tlacelel. It was unanimously agreed that
Tlacelel's game would be a great addi-
tion to the afternoon gathering.

During the conversation, with serving
pots emptied, a temple priest appeared
at the courtyard entrance, waiting for
Milintica's acknowledgment. A simple
nod allowed the priest to approach the
table. He was there to remind Milintica about upcoming sacrifices for the
approaching harvest season. Milintica
nodded in agreement and accompanied
the priest to the Templo Mayor. This
signaled for everyone else to depart. The
women stood up first to clear the table,
followed by the men, leaving the courtyard, each heading towards their desig-
nated city section.

A warm breeze swept across the island
under the blazing sun. Tlacelel stood
at the palace entrance, surveying his
surroundings, knowing he would soon

have the authority over everything. The weight of decision-making, ruling, protecting, and judging was about to fall on his shoulders. An anxious thrill washed over him as he recognized the honor and immense responsibility. After a final glance at the empire, with guards in place and everything in order, he walked back into the palace.

The harvesters prepared for the upcoming season in the city while the priests and temple leaders deliberated on sacrifices and forecasts for the year. Children joyfully ran and played in the streets as guards, like vigilant watchmen, stood along the perimeter. Suddenly, a glimmer of light captured the attention of a guard. He raised his hand and signaled towards the light, and with a warning shout, he notified the others of the sighting.

Twenty soldiers immediately ran toward the bridge and flanked it,
ten on either side. Two guards ran to alert Milintica, who then escorted him to the bridge. The source of the light, a shining man, was followed by four

others; two carried flags, the other two with their hands on their weapons. Milintica arrived on the scene and stood at the mouth of the bridge, accompanied by his warriors. Surprised by what he saw, Milintica walked toward the light that approached him and his empire.

Milintica took two steps closer, then stopped. He saw the fair skin and body that shone like the sun and said in reverence, "Quetzalcoatl." He knelt on one knee and bowed his head; everyone else did the same. The visitor stopped in his tracks. He stayed still for a moment, then walked toward the city. Milintica arose, called his warriors to ease, welcomed the guest, and guided the god Quetzalcoatl through the great city.

Milintica, knowing he was conversing with a deity, continued speaking without pausing to ensure the guest understood his words. Milintica ushered the god through the great city. He gestured in all directions, indicating the irrigation, aqueduct, temples, palace, and ultimately, the Templo Mayor, where Milintica mentioned they would conduct sacrifices later that day. As they proceeded, they circled the front and side of the temple, eventually arriving at the rear. Silently, they traversed a narrow path between the temple and the priests' lodgings. Upon reaching a set of stone stairs seemingly leading to nowhere, Milintica halted and altered his tone. Facing Quetzalcoatl, he disclosed, "This site is our most esteemed treasure dedicated to your honor. Few are aware of its existence. It is a confidential and religious secret. Showing you this place is a privilege."

Milintica put his right hand on his chest and gently lowered his head. Quetzalcoatl seemed to anticipate what was coming next because his eyes gleamed. Due to the sacred nature of the site, the flag bearers and two guards accompanying the god were instructed to remain behind. The six priests, each holding golden goblets filled with blood, led the way inside. Gradually, everyone else followed suit as they disappeared into the darkness.

Down the staircase they descended,

where the darkness grew more intense with each step. Quetzalcoatl proceeded cautiously, using the stone walls for support. Though the walls felt damp, the encompassing darkness required him to be aided by the wall to keep his stability. Suddenly, a spark appeared out of nowhere, breaking into dilated pupils. A radiant golden light, reflected by the mounds of golden coins, illuminated the chambers at the stairwell's end. Quetzalcoatl stood transfixed, his eyes wide open, taking in the vast rooms adorned with gold and precious gems such as onyx, opal, turquoise, and amber.

The priests stood around. The now-empty goblets were extended in front of them, their heads bowed. Quetzalcoatl looked all around and realized where the blood had been poured. He looked down at his hands, which were now stained with blood. The walls of the stairway still dripped with scarlet. To enter a sacred place, proof of sacrifice had to be given; if not, the person who entered empty-handed would be cursed. Worried about the blood on his hands and amazed by the amount of treasure in the chambers, Quetzalcoatl crossed his arms and placed his hands on his chest to wipe them dry. He left blood-stained prints on his body. The priests and all present took this as an acceptance of their treasures.

The priests raised their heads and walked toward the stairs. Before their departure, Milintica instructed them to prepare the sacrifices to be offered immediately in tribute to Quetzalcoatl's arrival. The priests consented and initiated the necessary arrangements. Milintica then directed his guards to accompany Quetzalcoatl's guards to the bridge, where they could await Quetzalcoatl.

Milintica guided Quetzalcoatl up the stairs, retracing their steps. The structures, streets, and surroundings appeared even more majestic to Quetzalcoatl as he reminisced and attempted to tally the gold in the chambers. They strolled around buildings and ascended a staircase until they reached a spot with a clear view of the top of the Templo Mayor. Milintica gestured for Quetzalcoatl to wait there. Anxiously, Quetzalcoatl nodded and sat down, unsure of what was to come.

Soon after, a conch shell trumpet sounded, and the streets quickly filled. Positioned at the peak of the Templo Mayor, the royal family gazed towards the city entrance. Quetzalcoatl also turned to observe. A pathway was cleared for a group of men bound together by a rope, guided by a warrior and two priests. The crowd erupted in cheers, showing gratitude by patting their shoulders as they passed through. The men tied to the rope gazed around in awe of the city. Trembling with fear, they ascended a staircase that wound from the left side of the temple, around the back, up the right side, and culminated at the summit. Clumped together, the men stood nervously, filled with dread.

The high priest went to the rooftop's center, where a stone table was placed. With both hands outstretched, he silenced the crowd. Quetzalcoatl, feeling anxious, attempted to clean the blood from his hands using whatever he could find nearby. The priest pointed to the group of men bound together. A guard untied the first man and severed the rope linking them. The audience erupted in cheers once more.

The first sacrifice was dragged to the altar. Struggling pointlessly, the man's eyes looked around for some comfort or mercy. He found none. The priest raised his obsidian blade as the temple servants stretched the body over the small stone table. Two priests held his legs, and two priests held his arms. Silence fell over the entire city as they awaited the plunge. In went the blade, and out came the heart of the sacrifice. The heart, still beating, was thrown into a golden pot on a burning woodpile. Like the still-alive sacrifice, the heart sizzled and cried out for mercy. The body of the sacrifice convulsed. The priests who held the legs now grabbed the arms, and the other two held his head as the high priest swung his arm with great force to decapitate the body. The group of men who were next to be sacrificed huddled a bit closer to each other. The city cheered as the priest held the head in the air, and the body was pushed down the steps of the Templo Mayor. This was repeated fourteen times with the other sacrifices. Each appeased Huitzilopochtli, the sun god, who promised a good harvest season.

After the last body met its severed head at the bottom of the stairs, everyone looked toward Quetzalcoatl. Unsure of what to do, he stood up, lifted his right hand in recognition, and everyone cheered. Quetzalcoatl made his way down the stairs to the main street. Through the cheers and bowing, he walked away from the temple, through the center road, over the bridge, across the grass field to the East, toward the woods and mountains. The sound of cheering faded away as he walked deeper into the woods. Cortes bent over and couldn't hold in his disgust any longer. Wiping his mouth, he motioned for his entourage to go ahead of him. They walked further into the woods, where the sound of their comrades grew. The rustling and the crackling of a branch made the men go silent. Everyone turned to face the sound; they saw Cortés and his men approaching, pale-faced and sweating. "Tenemos que destruir a estos animales" he said. It would have to be done later that same evening because there had to be an end to the slaughter and the waste of precious gold. Like most invaders, Cortés thought he knew best, and his men, ready to return to Spain, agreed with his erratic statements.

The royal family once again convened in the palace's courtyard in the city for dinner. The flowers looked even more vibrant in the setting sun's soft glow. Tlacelel's rabbit added to the sweet corn, tortillas, beans, and vegetable sauce aroma. Smiles were gleaming all around because Quetzalcoatl had honored them with a visit. Milintica told everyone how Quetzalcoatl was pleased with their city and that his eyes shone when he saw their most precious secret.

The meal was delicious, and spirits were high as the sunset light turned the courtyard red. Milintica looked up to examine the sky and suddenly stood up. This made everyone go silent. A loud bang, followed by screams of fear and a call to arms, caused everyone's attention to turn to the outside world.

The women got up and took the children to the back of the palace, where a small room for storage was located. The men rushed outside, ready to confront the chaos. Smoke, dust, and stones began to fill the air. Flashing lights were coming from every street. Bangs, crashes, and clanging couldn't muffle the screams and cries from women and children. Very quickly, the bangs were more constant than the clangs. Tlacelel did not know why Quetzalcoatl's guards attacked the city, but he ran faster than ever from the palace to the street. His hand was already on his sling, ready to release his first direct hit to the face of an unsuspecting soldier. Reminiscent of the rabbit, the invader turned on the spot and fell to the ground.

The Aztec warriors fought with all the courage and anger they could muster, but in vain. For what are arrows and stones against guns and armor? Despite the unbalanced odds,

Tlacalel's courage strengthened him, and his fighting intensified. One, two, three invaders were cut down. Four, then five, fell from the brute strength of a prince indignant at the murdering of his people. Six, seven, eight, nine. His bones and muscles were infused with the rage of the gods that demanded retribution in blood. Down the street, he ran toward the city's entrance, leaving a trail of offerings in his wake. Ten, eleven, and twelve now lay on the ground. Seeing a large group of raiders making their stand, he approached them in full force. As he got closer, their guns seemed to lower. Taking this as a sign, Tlacalel didn't slow his pace.

He grabbed his sling, and in a matter of seconds, he loaded and shot twice, aiming for their throats. CRACK! They fell to their knees, gasping for air. The others looked around, confused as to what was happening. All they saw was a man coming toward them with fire in his eyes and a black crown on his head. The crowned figure was upon them before they could regain their composure, striking, stabbing, and beating with great force. They fell to their deserved end. Tlacelel turned and looked toward his city. The screams and shouts seemed to have died down.

Victory or defeat, he did not know. Breathing heavily, he loosened his hair, his crown now a black cape lying stately on his shoulders and back. Blinking through drops of sweat, his eyes saw a flash of light, and then his ears heard a boom. His breath was taken away momentarily. He took a step back, and his left hand grasped his side. His hair moved slowly across his face with the wind. Blood dripped down his side from a bullet wound. His strength began to fail. Staggering to the edge of the banks of the lake, he fell on his knees facing the great city that an imposter and his scum had taken over.

Looking up into the sky, Tlacelel Montezuma took his last breath and fell back, lifeless, on the ground. His bloodstained hand was out by his side. His fingertips touched the water. Drops of blood streamed down his hand and painted the water all around—drop after drop, taken away by the stream.

The act of bravery and courage by Tlacelel satisfied the gods' vengeful demands, leading to an eternal curse bestowed upon foreigners. Whenever a foreigner drank water from any lake, river, or spring in Mexicali, they would fall ill, while a true Mexica would remain unharmed and be honored with the same black crown worn by Tlacelel. This tradition served as a testament to the lineage passed down through generations.

The grand empire collapsed, leaving behind the legacy of the Black Crown. Cortés and his men wasted and tainted Tenochtitlan's wealth and advances, but Montezuma's Revenge safeguarded the land against potential invaders and traitors.